MAN TIGER

Eka Kurniawan was born in Tasikmalaya, Indonesia in 1975. He studied philosophy at Gadjah Mada University, Yogyakarta. He has published several novels, including *Beauty Is a Wound* and *Man Tiger*, as well as short stories. His novels have been published in a number of languages, including English.

MAN TIGER

Eka Kurniawan

Translated by
Labodalih Sembiring

VERSO
London • New York

This English-language edition published by Verso 2015
Translation © Labodalih Sembiring 2015
Originally published in Bahasa Indonesia as *Lelaki Harimau*
© Gramedia Pustaka Utama, Jakarta 2004

7 9 10 8 6

Verso
UK: 6 Meard Street, London W1F 0EG
US: 20 Jay Street, Suite 1010, Brooklyn, NY 11201
www.versobooks.com

Verso is the imprint of New Left Books

ISBN-13: 978-1-78168-859-5
eISBN-13: 978-1-78168-860-1 (UK)
eISBN-13: 978-1-78168-861-8 (US)

British Library Cataloguing in Publication Data
A catalogue record for this book is available from the British Library

Library of Congress Cataloging-in-Publication Data
A catalog record for this book is available from the Library of Congress

Typset in Monotype Fournier by Hewer Text UK Ltd, Edinburgh
Printed and bound by CPI Group (UK) Ltd, Croydon, CR0 4YY

Introduction by Benedict Anderson

The most exhilarating part of literature's history is that it has no teleology and is not driven by the chariot of Progress. The most original writers seem like unexpected meteorites. Who could predict the arrival of Sophocles, Virgil, Lady Murasaki, Cervantes, Melville, Lu Hsün, Shakespeare, Proust, Gogol, Ibsen, Márquez, or Joyce? They are in one sense the product of their epochs and, in another, of the vernacular languages into which they were born and raised. But uncountable numbers lived at the same time, spoke the same languages and wrote nothing memorable. Class and education cannot explain their arrival. Their familial ancestors and descendants rarely show any substantive literary talents.

Eka Kurniawan is certainly Indonesia's most original living writer of novels and short stories, and its most unexpected meteorite. He was born on November 28, 1975, the day that the little ex-Portuguese colony East Timor declared its sovereign independence from Lisbon. On December 7, 1975, Pearl Harbour Day, President Gerald Ford and Henry Kissinger arrived in Indonesia to bless the tyrant Suharto's launching of a bloody occupation (using American weapons) to annex East Timor. Eka is proud of his birth-date because it marks the beginning of twenty-two years of stubborn resistance by the East Timorese that eventually forced Jakarta to abandon its cruel colonial rule.

For most of his first ten years he was in the care of his mother's parents in his birthplace, a tiny isolated village (without any road access) on the dangerous coast of the Indian Ocean in the southeast fringe of West Java. The grandparents were literate, but there were no books in their simple home. Little Eka got his early connection to "literature" via two village women and an invisible man. His grandmother loved to narrate the legends, the fairy tales, and the history of their village. An old lady (a distant relative, too), who lived alone, was a much more skilled storyteller. Almost every evening, after prayers at the local mosque, she gathered the village children on the porch of her house and enchanted them with uncountable magical tales. The invisible man was a storyteller on the radio who knew how to create different voices for the characters in his wider-ranging legends of West Java, an area mostly populated by the Sundanese (Central and East Java were dominated by the Javanese).

In 1984, the little boy was sent to join his parents and continue his primary schooling in Pangandaran, a small market town right on the border between Central and West Java, where a mixed population used mutually understandable vernacular Javanese and Sundanese. The town had no bookshop or municipal library. But Eka's father, who worked as a tailor and a creator of T-shirts for the occasional tourists, was in his way a proto-literary man. He had two contrasting sidelines. As leader of prayers he taught little Muslim boys to memorize parts of the Koran, even if they did not understand the Arabic. He also served as a part-time teacher of English at a local school, and from its skimpy library he would come home with books for his children. In his youth he had studied at a teacher's college, but never finished. Perhaps this was why in the evening he would compose sermons for the nearby mosque and write religious articles for various Muslim magazines (which, Eka says, he never read!). More important than all the above was Eka's early discovery of what were then called "gardens of books," one at the bus station and another behind the little seaside tourist hotel. In the gardens, vendors sold or rented out Indonesian horror and action comics, as well as the badly translated Nick Carter detective series and the romances of Barbara Cartland. Periodically, bicycling vendors would also stop at the family home to sell or rent out the same kind of reading matter. All this stimulated the eleven-year-old Eka to start writing poems, short stories and even sketches of novels.

He must have been a top pupil in Pangandaran's high school, since he was accepted, at the age of around seventeen, to Gadjah Mada University in Jogjakarta, the capital of the Republic of Indonesia during the revolutionary war against the Dutch colonialists from 1945 to 1949. The only opening for him was in the Faculty of Philosophy, even though he was not much interested in its courses. But to his amazement he found in the faculty's chaotic library *Growth of the Soil*, an English translation of one of the Norwegian Nobel Prize–winner Knut Hamsun's masterpieces. Addicted to haunting nearby flea-markets for used books, he later found Knut Hamsun's even more famous novel *Hunger*. Interestingly enough, in Gadjah Mada's general library there was a section devoted to American studies, donated by the

American Embassy, which to his surprise made room for English translations of the novels of García Márquez and Cervantes, Borges's short stories, and the books of some great Russians—Gogol, Tolstoy, Dostoyevsky, and Chekhov (maybe because the USSR had disappeared by that time). As one might predict, American studies also featured Faulkner, Hemingway, Welty, Steinbeck, and Toni Morrison, and, perhaps in a gesture to the UK, Salman Rushdie.

Eka records that he then read very little Indonesian literature. It is likely there were two reasons for this peculiarity. The first was that as a provincial "hick," he experienced culture-shock in the big city of Jogjakarta and in Gadjah Mada, which drew students from all over the vast Indonesian archipelago: so many religious affiliations, ethnicities, languages, customs, ambitions. In the library for American studies, he could leave behind the shock and fly to a global treasury, and very few young Indonesians knew English well enough to soar above him. The second was the philistine Suharto dictatorship (1966–98), which began with the massacre of hundreds of thousands of so-called Communists, constructed a gulag of political prisoners across the archipelago, and banned the circulation of any books regarded as leftist and subversive. Pramoedya Ananta Toer, Indonesia's grand novelist, composer of stunning short stories and memorable critical essays, spent fourteen years on the remote island prison of Buru without trial. After his release, all his works remained forbidden—Suharto's ban is today still formally in force, though in practice it is a dead letter.

In the 1990s, Gadjah Mada was still an old-fashioned liberal university, not yet commercialized, Americanized, or rating-ized. Students could stay students for years without being evicted, and theses at different levels were not tightly linked to the fortresses of the disciplines. Eka remained a student till 1998, while his earliest short stories began to be published in "Sunday newspapers" in Jakarta.

Nonetheless, in 1997, Eka decided to write his "philosophical" thesis on Pramoedya. Why did he make this choice? In 1996, the newspapers began to alert the reading public to the appearance of the PRD (People's Democratic Party) a semi-underground Marxist party, which attracted activist university students eager to work for Suharto's downfall. Eka recalls being in close touch with the PRD students in his faculty, though he was not interested in joining any party or political organization. One of the tasks of the Jogjakarta PRD was stealthily to circulate Pramoedya's gigantic Buru Tetralogy, composed in the gulag, on the origins and development of nationalism and socialism in Indonesia during the first quarter of the twentieth century. Eka got copies from a PRD friend and was enormously impressed and excited. In July 1997 the great Asian Financial Crash began in Thailand and moved on to Indonesia that September. In a few weeks, the rupiah sank from 2,500 per American dollar to 17,000. Many banks and businesses went bankrupt, unemployment vastly increased, and the economy was nearly in ruins. There followed a series of mass demonstrations, some organized by the PRD, demanding the end of the dictatorship. Eka told me that he joined all their demonstrations in Jogjakarta—his first political experience. The regime tried to defend itself with brutal crackdowns, during which many prominent activists were kidnapped, tortured, and often disappeared. "I presented my draft thesis on Pramoedya to my intimidated faculty teachers in early 1998, and of course it was rejected. But soon after the May riots in Jakarta that forced Suharto to resign, and his regime to collapse, I presented my draft once again, and this time it was easily accepted—of course!" Eventually, some good PRD friends found an activist publisher willing to publish his thesis under the title *Pramoedya Ananta Toer and the Literature of Socialist Realism*.

Much later, when Eka wrote a short reply to a question about which Indonesian writers impressed him the most, he said he had a melancholy three. The first was Amir Hamzah, Indonesia's finest poet and a pro-independence aristocrat in Northern Sumatra, executed during the Revolution of 1945–49 by gangsters masquerading as revolutionaries. Second came Pramoedya, and third Widji Tukul, a brave new kind of radical Javanese poet, who was disappeared, probably by the seasoned killers commanded by Lt. General Prabowo, once Suharto's son-in-law, with maniacal ambitions to become the country's president. (Fortunately, he was defeated in the national election of 2014 by Djoko Widodo, the much-loved young governor of Jakarta, and the first presidential candidate unsullied by the brutal and corrupt Suharto regime.)

In Indonesia, as everywhere else in our world, serious studies of authors and their works are typically left to drudges in departments of history and literary criticism, thanks to the usual egotism of creative writers or the cliques to which they are attached. Young Eka is a rare exception to this rule. His book is affectionately admiring of Pramoedya's political courage and innovations in Indonesian letters, but he argued that socialist realism was a passé literary form. Unfortunately, his analysis was almost entirely based on the Buru Tetralogy.

What was not accessible to him at the time were the great collections of Pramoedya's short stories from the 1950s, which are far from socialist realism and full of magical realism *avant la lettre*.

In 2000 Eka published his first collection of short stories, cheekily titled *Graffiti in the Toilet*, and two years later the huge novel *Beauty Is a Wound*. The pair, utterly different in many ways, immediately made him a literary star in Indonesia. The short-story collection showed his skill as a black humorist and satirist of his own generation (including PRD leaders who soon became power-hungry opportunists), and his technical mastery of the conjunction of the oral tales of his childhood village and the bourgeois culture of the post-Suharto big cities. At the other extreme, *Beauty Is a Wound* is a quasi-historical novel stretching from the late colonial period, through the Japanese Occupation, the Revolution of 1945–49, the long extremist Islamic rebellion of the 1950s, the rise and bloody downfall of the Indonesian Communist Party, and the early Suharto dictatorship. But the setting is not national or even regional: it is an unnamed little town close to the Indian Ocean. Nothing is documented, and everything is suffused with magic, traditional and newly created legends, and confusing oral histories.

Eka once told me that *Beauty Is a Wound* was born out of three earlier novels, which he decided to agglomerate, with many difficulties, into a vast single tome. One could imagine that consciously or unconsciously it grew out of his criticism of Pramoedya's socialist realism, and perhaps even challenges the old man's well-known tetralogy, translated into many languages.

Then in 2004 came *Lelaki Harimau*, translated here with

the slightly awkward title *Man Tiger*. As in *Beauty Is a Wound*, the setting is an unnamed township near the Indian Ocean and its rural environs. But this time the novel is relatively short and is tightly and elegantly constructed. The story largely focuses on the tragedy of two interlinked and tormented families over two generations. The hero Margio is an ordinary half-urban, half-village youngster, who nonetheless is possessed by a supernatural female white tiger, inherited from his much-loved grandfather. In many parts of Indonesia there are ancient tales about magical male tigers who protect good villages or families. But they are external and reside in jungles. Eka borrowed from these old stories, but his tiger is female and is inside Margio and only sometimes under his control. I will not here describe the content of *Man Tiger*, allowing the reader the privilege of suspense.

Instead, let me make some observations on the most important characteristics of Eka's evolving style, which makes him quite unlike any other living Indonesian novelist. The first is the sheer beauty of his prose and the vast expanse of his vocabulary, which includes contemporary coinages as well as many obscure words, still used in remote villages, but absent in present-day urban-centered dictionaries. The second is the pervasive voice of the storyteller, which rarely has the characters speak, and when they do it is only for a few sentences. The storyteller is a complete unknown—the reader learns nothing about her or his age, gender, occupation, or location—just as with the oral storytellers of the past. The third is a growing discipline in the use of the supernatural. In *Beauty Is a Wound*, the magical is everywhere, as it is in the still popular traditional puppet theater based on local versions of the Mahabharata and Ramayana epics. In this theater there is always a zoo of gods and goddesses, aristocratic warriors, devils, kings, giants, clowns, ghosts, princesses, and so on, all of whom are iconographically fixed. For example, princesses and queens are always prodigiously beautiful, while the female clowns are physical grotesques. There are no plain-but-fascinating women. In the earlier of Eka's two novels, women are always either "too beautiful to believe" or horribly ugly. But in *Man Tiger* there is only one supernatural being, and space is made for ordinary women whose characters develop as the story proceeds. The fourth development is a better grasp on chronology. In *Man Tiger*, the chapters are marked by well-planned shifts in time, without being flashbacks. The first pages are almost simultaneous with the last. In *Beauty Is a Wound* there are a great number of time-shifts but they often seem arbitrary and needlessly confusing. Finally, sex. The earlier novel has plenty of sex, but the scenes are flattened out by too much supernaturalism in the manner of the shadow puppet theater. In *Man Tiger* the sex is often brutal and deceptive, and the tragic plot hinges on this fact. Eka's decision to make his supernatural white tigers female, and put them at the side of human males alone, is an innovation that allows for different readings of the novel, which is now three-dimensional, rather than two-dimensional in the manner of stories from antiquity. The purport of these comments on Eka's mature style is to underline his many-sided originality in seamlessly melding the old and the new. No wonder that two of his favorite writers are Gogol and Melville.

MAN TIGER

A NOVEL

EKA KURNIAWAN

One

On the evening Margio killed Anwar Sadat, Kyai Jahro was
blissfully busy with his fishpond. A scent of brine wafted
through the coconut palms, the sea moaned at a high pitch,
and a gentle wind ruffled the algae, coral trees and lantanas.
The pond lay in the middle of a cacao plantation, the trees
barren from lack of care, their fruit shriveled and thin, like
bird's eye chilis. The leaves were of use only to the tempeh
factories, which collected them every night. Through this
plantation ran a creek full of snakeheads and eels, its overflow swelling the swamp around it. Not long after the
plantation was declared bankrupt, people had arrived to put
up boundary stakes, clear away the water hyacinths and vast
tangles of *kangkong*, and plant the marsh with rice. Kyai
Jahro had come with them, but had grown rice for only one
season. Rice required too much attention and time. Jahro,
who had never heard of Orion—the short-season cultivar—
replaced his rice with peanuts, which were more resilient and
less trouble. At harvest time his fields yielded two sacks of
pods that made him wonder how he would ever eat them all.
So he turned his parcel of marsh into a pond and threw in
some *mujair* and *nila* fry, and it became his favorite pastime

to feed his fish before sundown, to watch them mouthing at the brimming water's surface.

He was spreading bran from the rice mill, as well as cassava and papaya leaves, on the water where his fish bobbed animatedly, when a motorcycle roared in the distance. He knew the sound so well he didn't bother to turn his head. It was even more familiar than the sound of the surau's drum that beat five times a day. It was Major Sadrah's shiny, bright-red Honda 70, which carried its owner to the surau, or brought his wife to the market, and at other times simply glided through the neighborhood in late afternoons, spinning around quiet corners when Sadrah had nothing else to do.

He was past eighty, Major Sadrah, but still in good shape. He had retired from the military many years ago, but every Independence Day stood among his fellow veterans. The city government was said to have given him a plot of land in the heroes' cemetery as a reward for his service, something he described as an invitation to die quickly. He swerved on his motorcycle and halted by the dike. After killing the engine, he wiped his mouth, above which lowered a dark mustache, for without this gesture he would not feel like himself. Jahro did not look up until Major Sadrah stood by his side. They talked about the previous night's rainstorm, which fortunately hadn't come during the herbal tonic company's film screening at the soccer field, although it must have nearly broken the hearts of every pond owner.

A similar rainstorm had come months ago, lasting one whole week. The creek, normally more mud than water, rose six feet, sweeping hosts of geese downstream, until the ponds around it disappeared. The fish, which would have filled the bellies of the villagers and their children, disappeared almost entirely. When the water subsided, all that was left were snails and the stems of banana plants. Jahro looked at Major Sadrah and said he had prepared some nets to cover his ponds and protect the fish in future.

At that moment, an old man on a bicycle, stooping to avoid the cacao branches above, called out to Jahro. Ma Soma, who taught children how to read the Koran at the surau, jumped off just in time to stop the bike hitting the dike. With both fists still firm on the handlebars, the bicycle reared up, like a horse yanked by its reins. Panting, he told them that Margio had killed Anwar Sadat. He said it in a manner suggesting that Jahro should hasten to lead the funeral prayers, for this had been one of his duties these past years.

"By God," said Major Sadrah. For a moment they exchanged baffled glances, as if it were a joke they couldn't understand. "This afternoon I saw him carrying that war relic of an old, rusty samurai sword. Darned kid, I hope he didn't get it back after I'd confiscated the damn thing."

"He didn't," said Ma Soma. "The kid bit through his jugular."

No one had ever heard of such a thing. There had been twelve murders over the past ten years in the city, and all involved machetes or swords. The cause of death was never a gun or kris dagger, and certainly not biting. People attacked with their teeth, particularly when women fought each other, but they didn't die that way. The identity of the killer and his victim made the news all the more shocking. They knew Margio the teenager and old Anwar Sadat all too well. It would never have occurred to anyone that these two figures

3

would feature in such a tragic drama, no matter how eager Margio was to kill someone, or how detestable the man named Anwar Sadat.

A few moments slipped by as they pondered, as if lost in thoughts of rancid blood burbling from a punctured neck and a teenage boy staggering in panic, stupefied by his own reck-lessness, his mouth and teeth red, like the snout of an ajak dog after its morning kill. These imaginary scenes were too astonishing to believe. Even the pious Kyai Jahro neglected to whisper *innalillahi*, while Sadrah mouthed indistinct words and forgot to wipe his gaping mouth. Ma Soma was getting tired of standing there, and turned his bicycle around, giving them a sign to hurry, and so they set off, becoming all the more panic-stricken, as if the murder had not yet taken place and they were going to thwart it.

It was true that while Sadrah was on his way home from prayers at the surau that afternoon, still wearing a sarong, he had noticed the boy carrying the samurai sword from the hut where the nightwatch stood vigil. Everyone now was talking about that sword as proof that he had long harbored an inten-tion to kill. The nightwatch hut stood in the middle of the village, opposite a defunct and overgrown brick factory. The samurai sword hung from the boy's hand as he plodded about, scarring the ground with its tip. At another moment he sat on a bench, swinging the sword, hitting the slit wooden drum used to sound the alarm. Several people saw this, but paid no heed. The sword was so worn out and rusty, it couldn't decapitate the scrawniest chicken.

Decades after the end of the war, the many samurai swords left behind by the Japanese had become decorations or talis-mans. Most of them were neglected and eaten away by the salty air, as Sadrah recalled. Perhaps Margio had found his sword at the dump or tucked away inside the brick factory. Sadrah noticed it and didn't overlook the fact that, no matter how damaged, it was still a sword, although he didn't seriously suspect that the boy intended to put an end to Anwar Sadat's life. There were no signs that they were at odds, as far as their neighbors knew.

He asked for the samurai sword mainly because he was worried that Margio was drunk on white sticky-rice arak and spoiling for a fight. These kids liked to get drunk, and that was the source of countless petty problems. He couldn't kill anyone with that worn-out sword, but drunkenness might push him to beat a neighbor's dog, then the neighbor might throw a rock at him in return, and things would get out of hand. Moreover, at last night's herbal tonic company's film screening at the soccer field, a crowd had gathered, an event which always threatened to unleash the fighting demon that lurked among the boys. The violence could drag on into the next day and often for days afterward. Whatever the case, Sadrah had good reason to worry about an unsheathed samurai sword being carried around at a roadside, no matter how harmless the object might seem.

"Why?" Margio asked, unwilling to hand over his toy. "Look, it's just a useless old piece of iron."

"But you could kill someone with it if you wanted," Sadrah said.

"That's my plan."

Even though the boy had clearly said he meant to commit murder, Sadrah paid no heed. He coaxed the kid, and after threatening to take him to the military headquarters, he managed to get the sword, took it home, and tossed it on top of the dog cage behind the house.

He soon forgot about the rusty sword, and saw no hint of the disaster to come. Perhaps age had made him complacent. Now he felt slightly sorry for having confiscated the useless sword. Had the shabby weapon remained with Margio, Anwar Sadat might still be alive. No matter how many times it struck him, he would have suffered no worse than bruises and broken bones. Now the Major shivered, imagining how the boy embraced Anwar Sadat as his jaws bit down on his neck.

That afternoon he had told the boys to take a break and chase women, if they had to, and make sure they had someone to have fun with that weekend. The next day he would take them boar hunting as usual. During the hunting season, they were good enough to stay sober on Saturday nights, other-wise they wouldn't be invited or even worse they'd end up impaled on a boar's tusks. They would go to the shore in troops, dragging wild women along, or greeting respectable ladies with bags of oranges and shy smiles. They would go home before ten o'clock, all sweet and obedient in the name of boars, and stay fast sleep until the call to prayer woke them at dawn. Darned kid, Major Sadrah cursed as he thought of Margio, for instead of resting and preparing himself for the coming boar hunt, he had gone to the house of the bristly, porcine Anwar Sadat and killed him.

Boar hunting had become their pastime many years ago, back when Sadrah was still the town's military commander. Anwar Sadat himself had always been highly enthusiastic every time the harvest season ended, when people were no longer bound to the soil, which was left fallow temporarily.

Although he had never raised a spear or run up and down the hills, he always provided boxed meals of rice and fried egg and a truck to take the hunters to the jungle's edge. Three times a year they enjoyed this sport, going on the season's non-stormy Sundays. Between hunts they would tame ajaks and train them to course their prey.

Among the troop of hunters that until recently had been under Sadrah's leadership, Margio was the champ. On his back he wore a scar from a slashing boar's tusk, and all his friends knew how many hogs had surrendered to the swings of his spear, before being dragged to the trap and shut up alive. They had no interest in a dead hog. Even when confronted by a raging boar, they would balk from killing it. They would wound it, just a little, before forcing it into to the trap. They didn't want the hogs to die, because they would later throw them into battle with the ajaks, in a public spectacle at the end of the hunting season. During these strategic hunts for these stupid beasts, Margio became known as the herder, with his powerful strides and ruthless spear. Not many had the courage to take up that role, running alongside the boar, matching its pace. It was a feat that earned Margio the admiration of his companions.

A few weeks earlier, Sadrah had been dismayed to learn that Margio had disappeared. Gone and nobody knew where. Some of his friends went looking for him on the shore, where he had often disappeared to pull up nets or hunt for stingrays with the fishermen, but no one there had seen him. For the two previous weeks, a circus had encamped by the soccer field, and everyone finally concluded that Margio most likely had joined the performers, moving from town to town. The idea sent Sadrah, who was ready with the vicious ajaks to welcome the boar-hunting season, into panic. As herder, Margio was irreplaceable. The first hunt the previous week had ended in disappointment. They had trapped only two boars and mostly because of the ajaks' agility. On that same day they heard that Margio's father had died.

His name was Komar bin Syueb, and his death brought his missing son home. No one was happier on his return than Sadrah, who had been heartbroken by failure of the hunt. But Sadrah dared not invite him to return to the jungle the following Sunday, out of respect for the mourning period. When the hunters jumped off their truck, with two squealing pigs in a cage, and dozens of hounds bound to each other by leather leashes, Margio showed up. He waved at them, jaunty despite the fact of his father waited to be buried.

Not long after the funeral, Margio came to Sadrah's house. He patted the hounds in the backyard with affection. He squatted there, cuddling the beasts one by one, scrubbing wax from their ears, and letting the animals bite the hem of his pants and his flip-flops. His face showed not a trace of grief. Instead he looked incredibly happy, as if he had unexpectedly won a big bet.

Major Sadrah had long known that the boy didn't get along with his father, and even suspected he wanted the old man dead. He had known the family since they first came to the village, and Margio was just a snotty child with a bag of marbles with which he enticed the other children into playing with him. Sadrah also got to know the father, and had seen the brutal man beat the child for the smallest of offenses. Now his father was gone, the ingenuous kid couldn't hide his joy, Sadrah thought, and when Margio saw him approaching, without hesitation he asked whether there would be a hunt the next week. He wanted to join in, even if he had to bring his own lunch and give up his place as herder.

But of course Sadrah gave him back his position.

Well, it was now clear he wouldn't be there next Sunday to herd the boars. Wretched kid, Sadrah thought. Earlier, when he was carrying the sword home, propping it on his shoulder with his legs wrapped in a sarong, feeling as if he were living in the war-torn era of the caliphs, it never occurred to him that Margio would join in if there were a fight. The boys fought a lot, drunk or sober. They were always eager to start throwing punches at the slightest provocation: an inadvertent collision at a *dangdut* show, a head blocking the view of a movie screen, or the sight of a girl they liked walking with another man. Living in a generally more peaceful period in the Republic's history, in which the business of war was left to soldiers, made these boys reckless. During the years when Sadrah commanded the town's soldiers, stopping these fights occupied him more than anything else. But as far as he knew, Margio was never a figure in this violence, despite everyone knowing his strength.

He was a kid who didn't like staying at home, but he was well behaved. He wasn't stupid enough to waste his time brawling, and during the day he would do odd jobs and spend the money he made on cigarettes and beer. He was moody, but sweet nonetheless. Everyone knew he hated his father and thought he was capable of finishing him off, but he never tried anything like that. He was absolutely not a trouble-maker. When Sadrah heard Margio had killed a man, he could not believe it.

He was so convinced the kid was harmless he had soon forgotten that Margio had said he wanted to kill someone.

When evening approached, after he had fed the hounds with fried giblets from the slaughterhouse, he took the Honda 70 out. He had gotten the motorbike years ago from a local police chief and didn't have any papers or a license plate, but luckily he had never once got a ticket. The police chief had probably confiscated the bike from a crook, and for months no one claimed it, and then it became Sadrah's. There were a lot of appropriated motorbikes, and the police chief had since offered Sadrah newer models, but he stayed faithful to his old favorite. Maybe it was the old-fashioned look that he liked, even though it often broke down and was louder than a rice mill.

Without a helmet and wearing only flip-flops, he would roar about the township and head out for the shore and the paddy fields, taking the path through the plantation. He liked the evening breeze, admired the landscape, and greeted the people he passed along the road. Once in a while he would drop by the repair shop to get someone to tune up the machine, and at other times he would stop by a stall and ask for a glass of coffee, before resuming his tour with a pipe that puffed out more smoke than his bike's exhaust. He was only going to stop by for a moment when he spotted Jahro by his pond. Then the evening jaunt was cut short by the news brought by Ma Soma.

Major Sadrah hurried toward his motorbike, which leant against a coconut tree, mounted it, and tried to kick-start the engine, always a problem. Several times it fired up only to die. Finally, getting a chance when the engine came on, he turned the gas up, making a clatter that sounded like a tin drum. He signaled the kyai, a teacher of the Koran, to climb on behind him, worried that the engine might conk out again.

Kyai Jahro was soon firmly seated behind the Major, after washing his hands and feet at the spout, and throwing what was left of the bran into his pond. Trailing along the bumpy path, slippery from last night's rain, the motorcycle felt frailer than a feverish donkey. The weight of two men was such a strain on the engine they had help it along now and then by pushing with their feet. The bike picked up speed as it arrived at a straight, flat road by the soccer field, and was followed at a distance by Ma Soma on his vintage bicycle.

"Stealing chickens, that's the only bad thing the boy ever did," Jahro said. "And the chickens were his father's."

It was no secret. Everyone in the village knew Margio often stole his father's chickens, not because he needed them, but out of spite. "I have no idea what was in the boy's mind that he could think of gnawing on someone's neck," said Sadrah.

Anwar Sadat himself now lay motionless under a brown batik cloth on the floor of his usually bright living room, now gloomy with unforgiving sorrow and echoing the undulating sobs of the women. The cloth was soaked with red, and curved to the contours of the corpse, while blood still flowed across the floor. Dark and clotted. No one dared to pull apart the curtain that divided the worlds of the living and the dead, for they were aware of the gaping wound, grimmer than any ghost. Just the thought of it made people nauseous and they would back away from the body.

Two policemen arrived in a patrol car. Its red light kept swirling even after the siren had been killed. They both froze by the door, the only people who'd had the chance to turn down the cloth, just for a second, before putting it back. Now they felt like an integral part of the event, though they had no reason to stay. Anwar Sadat's wife hadn't let them take the body away for a postmortem, which was reasonable. There was no mystery about the cause of death or the killer. Anwar Sadat didn't need to be examined, and the only things that would be granted to him were the ritual washing, the covering of his wound with cotton wool, prayers, and an immediate interment.

It appeared that he wouldn't be buried until the next morning. Maharani, his youngest daughter, was away at college and would not make it back before dawn. The fact the girl had been home last night only added to the drama. She had been there the whole week during her long holiday, before she suddenly took off that morning. People imagined the tragedy spreading all the way to Maharani's lodgings, the girl still exhausted and unpacking. She would have to return all her belongings to her backpack or leave them behind altogether, exiting in tears and bearing a thousand questions, for she'd left her father in good health. No one had told her it was murder. There was just a short message that he had died, and now the girl was probably hurrying to catch the next bus or train home.

At the house of mourning, groups of women flocked into the front yard and the terrace, whispering to each other and cooking up their own versions of what had happened. Five oil palm trees and a starfruit tree decorated the spacious yard where little children liked to swing on a tire that dangled from a branch. By the roadside a majestic flame tree shed petals that scattered on a carpet of Japanese stiltgrass, on which small children would play-fight and roll around and where a raft of turkeys roamed. At each of two corners was a pond, with fat goldfish and lotus plants and little splashing fountains. On the edges and in the middle of these ponds were a number of stone sculptures: semi-nude women doing hand laundry and children swimming, all produced by Anwar Sadat's very own skillful hands.

Another of his artworks familiar to the neighbors was a wooden slit drum in the shape of a penis, hanging in front of the house. It functioned as a bell for guests. Years ago he had arrived as an art institute graduate, selling paintings by the beach, before getting married and settling in the village. He always said that he was an admirer of Raden Saleh, and displayed his own reproductions of the great painter's work in his house, including the famous tiger and bison fight, shamelessly imitating the man's techniques. He was not at all bothered by the fact that his artistic reputation was known only among the people around his house.

He married a trainee midwife, who once dropped by and asked him to paint her portrait. Anwar Sadat made the girl look far more beautiful than she had ever really been, and she fell in love with him for that. Not wanting to break the girl's heart, he married her instantly, later to find himself very rich as the girl was heiress to half the township's land. Ater that he was no longer so eager to pursue artistic fame of any sort, owing to the inheritance of his wife who also worked as a midwife at the hospital. But of course he still painted and made sculptures, mostly portraits of people he knew, and impeccable copies of Raden Saleh's masterpieces. Save for a portrait of Major Sadrah in the man's own house, his canvases collectively displayed a myriad of beautiful women.

He really had no job after he gave up painting professionally. He spent his boundless free time playing chess with Sadrah, sponsoring the village soccer club, and chasing girls.

The last of these habits, the pursuit and seduction of girls, and sometimes widows or willing wives, was done with more passion than he ever put into his painting. This too was no secret, because a secret couldn't stay long in the mouth of any of his neighbors. Even so, the immoral impression he gave never eclipsed people's respect for him, and at every meeting they would let him give lengthy speeches, and he always turned out to be an eloquent speaker. He was charming, and for that reason people forgave him. Plus there was the fact that few of his friends could honestly claim to be better behaved.

That morning nobody had seen the grim reaper resting on his shoulder. Anwar Sadat was a jolly devil who never looked glum, as if death might never touch him. As usual he went to the pancake stall for breakfast, where he jostled with teenagers in school uniform looking worried as they waited for the school bell. Anyone there would have heard jokes from his fried-tempeh-and-pancake-stuffed mouth. Anwar Sadat would have been sitting on the small bench, before the smoldering stove, while the vendor poured batter into the griddle on the stove, turning the fritters over and over in a wok full of boiling oil. He would have pinched the chins of girls in school uniform until they protested at the lewdness, and pulled to one side to avoid his sudden attempt to peck at their cheeks.

They would remember him clearly, wearing plain white shorts and an undershirt bearing the ABC jewelry store logo. He was chubby and a little sluggish, due to age and lack of exercise, yet he would brag that his cock was as solid as a horn, and never concealed his explosive lust. That morning he talked a lot, worrying about his youngest child, who had

14

given no reason for her decision to leave when she was still on holiday, carrying her bag to the bus station alone, refusing to be seen off.

The previous night, after watching the movie at the soccer field, the girl would not talk to anyone. She wouldn't touch her dinner nor watch television as she usually did, and the entire night there wasn't so much as a peep from her radio, something she normally enjoyed. She didn't even leave her bedroom to go to the bathroom, and Anwar Sadat was puzzled that she didn't perform the dawn prayers, since his youngest child was quite pious. She came out of her room that morning, still not talking and tears in her eyes. Anwar Sadat had no idea what had happened, and he was afraid that if he asked she would only snap at him. He wondered whether he'd done something wrong. The young girl simply walked past him, carrying her towel to the bathroom. And something out of the ordinary happened yet again, as Maharani was out again in only a moment. She went back to her room and made herself up simply, as if she believed that she was as beautiful as she should be. But then she came out holding a bag, ate nothing for breakfast, and said brusquely, "I have to go."

In retrospect, her dejected eyes and cheerless face seemed to hint that her father was going to die that afternoon. Yet she left Anwar Sadat in a hurry, insisting on going alone to the bus station, as though they would have lots of time to see each other in the future. At the pancake stall he couldn't stop grumbling about Maharani, not with any real sense of grievance, but rather as an excuse to boast about his daughter.

Anwar Sadat had three daughters, all born in the early

years of his marriage when he and his wife had enough fire between them to exhaust one another in bed. Years later, when their love had waned, people began to forget his wife's name, Kasia, and simply called her Mrs. Midwife. Anwar Sadat was lucky to have no children by his other women. Bastard children would always be more of a curse to the father's family than to the mother's. His promiscuity was passed on to his children, as was his good looks.

His looks had enthralled a lot of girls over the years, and Anwar Sadat was handsome even in old age, when his body ballooned and his hair dwindled to patches. Even then, he drew the attention of adventurous would-be lovers. His fine looks were an astonishing contrast to those of his wife. With a nose like a parrot's beak, thick jaw, and cold patrician manners, Kasia was more the witch than the princess. It wasn't so much that she was exceptionally ugly, but she was definitely unattractive to the majority of men. There was a widespread conviction that the failed artist had married money, and with her money he could afford to sleep with a lot of women, most of whom his wife knew about, though she chose not to care, so long as he didn't get any of them pregnant.

The eldest daughter, Laila, inherited her father's sex appeal and lewd temperament. She was beautiful and full figured with a flawless, dewy complexion. Her face betrayed more than a little arrogance. By the age of sixteen, she was an exceptionally curvaceous schoolgirl, and a target for the boys as well as the teachers, until one day her father found out she was pregnant. Anwar Sadat searched frantically for a shaman to remove what was in her belly. His wife wouldn't help, and the school would not accept a pregnant pupil. As soon as she graduated, Anwar Sadat dragged her and the classmate said to be responsible to a *penghulu*, who could officiate at the wedding. Two days later, the newlywed husband found her in bed with another man.

It became the town's most sensational scandal. Anwar Sadat went red in the face at the slightest allusion to what happened, and Kasia disappeared for several days to a relative's house. Both men, the husband and the adulterer, gave up on her after that. People started referring to her as the Widow, and when they saw her whispered, "She's easy."

Maesa Dewi, the middle sister and the most beautiful, was cut from a different cloth. She was not as curvaceous as the eldest, and possessed a mysteriously tender manner. She comported herself with more respect for propriety, a surface quality that outlived her father by many years. That was just the way she was. At school, her reports praised her intelligence—an achievement her sisters never matched. Maesa Dewi finished school without a blemish on her record. His little remaining moral sense gave Anwar Sadat enough insight to make him love and admire the girl, who, unlike her elder sister, never shared his lascivious nature. Confident she was still a virgin, her father agreed to let her go to university. He then managed to persuade his wife to sell a plot of land to raise the money for her education, even though Kasia no longer believed any one of her three daughters was mentally sound. When the Sweet One unexpectedly returned after a year, she brought back not a diploma, but a newborn baby and a jobless boyfriend she later married. No one whispered that she was easy. She seemed to be faithful. Nonetheless, the stories of the eldest and middle daughers created a notion among those who thought of themselves as moral that all three of them were wicked and out of control.

They bet that one day Maharani, the youngest sister, would bring home a newborn, no matter how much evidence they saw that this would be wholly out of character.

At the pancake stall, after her sudden departure, he could not stop talking about Maharani. He spoke of the small items she had brought home. Maharani left her father a penknife, a large comb for her curly-haired mother, and a music box for her little nephew. Anwar Sadat retold his daughter's jokes, even though some people had heard them straight from Maharani's mouth throughout the holiday. Kasia tried to stop this exaggerated prattling, and the other two daughters didn't conceal their burning jealousy, but it was Margio who finally put an end to it.

Now Anwar Sadat lay dead, waiting for his grave to be dug, for the bier to be cleaned, and most of all for his youngest daughter to return and witness the ghastly wound before sobbing more powerfully than Kasia, Laila, and Maesa Dewi combined. Anyone looking at them would see Kasia more disheveled than usual, on her knees, biting one end of a cloth coiling onto her lap. Why she brought the cloth was a mystery. Next to her was Laila the Widow, trying in vain to console her mother, despite having recently lost consciousness herself, only coming to her senses when someone sprinkled water on her face. Most shaken of all was Maesa Dewi, the first to see Anwar Sadat's nearly detached head. Still howling with grief, as if her belly were full of boiling water, she folded her arms around her baby, whose crying nearly matched her own.

The other female mourners accompanied the four women's grieving with softer, more subdued cries, like a choir that harmonized on different levels of grief. Their eyes were swollen and livid, visibly strained by sadness for the loss of this callous and unfaithful individual. And since Ma Soma, after wandering around the surau, had found the body, carried it from the crime scene, and then covered it with a batik cloth, none of these women had taken proper care of the dead man. Meanwhile Ma Soma fetched his bicycle and set off to find Kyai Jahro. He had found the cloth in the artist's studio, the dyed patterns designed by the victim himself. That it would be used to wrap his corpse had never crossed Anwar Sadat's mind. Soon Jahro and Sadrah arrived, and people looked at them with eyes that seemed to beg for either mercy or help. Kyai Jahro, the Koran teacher, was related to Anwar Sadat's wife, and he immediately took control.

He and Sadrah carried the body, without removing the batik shroud, from the house to the front yard, leaving a shadowy reddish trail behind. He weighed eighty kilos, Major Sadrah thought, if he'd been a boar the ajaks would have ripped him apart. They took the corpse to a stool by the well, where Ma Soma had placed a pile of towels, sulphur soap, a bowl of water, flower petals, and of course borax. It was there that the kyai finally pulled down the cloth, slowly, bracing himself for the shock. With several men as witnesses, the hidden secret was now exposed. The Istighfar prayer slid from the kyai's mouth, begging Allah for forgiveness over and over, while the other men, following his example, mumbled as they stared at the ragged wound on the pallid neck. They saw how the blood still flowed in fizzing bubbles. The scene was nauseating—more terrifying than any nightmare—and several of the men turned away.

Stimulated by a childish curiosity, Sadrah examined the body, hoping to find out more of what Margio had done.

19

True enough an artery had been severed, dangling like the cable in a shattered radio. More savage than I imagined, he thought, seeing that the neck was almost cut in two, as if the butcher hadn't quite finished his task.

"His father died a few days ago, following his little sister, who passed away a week after her birth," Jahro said. "I think the kid's gone mad."

"He was crazy to have bitten a man like that," said Sadrah.

The air became cold and Major Sadrah could hear from a distance his ajaks howling, asking to be caged, or more probably they had caught the smell of blood on the evening breeze in their carnivorous snouts. Before darkness descended, Jahro asked some people to bring buckets of water. The pumps whirred noisily as water spouted out. After vanishing for a while, Ma Soma reappeared carrying bags of cotton-wool balls. Jahro washed the wound himself, very solemnly, believing he could stop the unremitting stream of red, as if the fearsome gash was a child's graze. He continued to mutter prayers. Sadrah, who had been through the brutal gauntlet of guerrilla warfare and seen bodies blown to bits by mortar fire, was genuinely awestruck by Jahro's chilly composure. He almost proposed leaving the gash as it was, to remind the kyai that the corpse would eventually rot in its grave.

The kyai's hands were still dancing, receiving balls of cotton and pressing them down, their color changing in an instant, before he bandaged the wound up and hid it under a muslin sheet. The wound now looked like a small cut on a living person, with the coiling muslin like a necklace. While he worked, other people stripped the body of clothes, bathed it, scrubbing it clean, and made it smell of flowers. There was a whiff of borax rising from the corpse, wafting around their heads.

Ma Soma brought a shroud from the surau, and then the body was wrapped up where they had been working.

"It's not befitting," said Kyai Jahro, "to leave him naked all night long," adding, "if the girl Maharani wants to see her father's head, we can still undo the knot of the shroud. But if she has any idea of what he looks like, she may not want to see him. Her mother and sisters will have lost their appetite for days, they'll have nightmares for the rest of their lives."

Now night had fallen, bringing with it cold and silence. Three people quickly carried the corpse into the surau, and people got ready to perform the funeral rites after the usual Maghrib prayers.

Despite his obsession with women, Anwar Sadat was a regular visitor to the surau. Even when he was busy, which was often, he would never forget to attend for the five daily prayers. Usually he would be the one who beat the big drum, and recited the *adhan* or the *iqama*. No one would trust him with the role of imam. His pious habits arose partly from the fact that most of his wife's relatives were active members of the surau, some of them hadjis or kyais. Another explanation was his sense of responsibility, since the surau stood on his grounds, built by his father-in-law years before Anwar Sadat arrived to sell his paintings. For all the right reasons, nobody believed he was really close to God.

The murder, as everyone came to believe, took place at exactly ten past four, because ten minutes before that Margio had been with some of his friends, and ten minutes later he was back with them, in a shocking state. They were gathering at the soccer field to watch people gamble on the pigeon

21

racing, and there was a great din from their shouting and whistling. Children competed with their pigeons, which would not return if they went farther than the village border, and therefore were let loose only from one side of the soccer field to chase a pigeon hen waved in a kid's hand on the far side. The best pigeons flew in from neighboring villages, following speeding motorcycle taxis, flitting by the clouds, before swooping down at the sight of the hen. Ten minutes before the murder Margio was there, lying on the grass staring at the sky.

Laila was there too, in fact she talked to him. She had a suspicion that Maharani's sudden departure had something to do with Margio, because she had seen them together every day that week. The previous night it was Margio who had gone with her to the movie screened by the herbal tonic company. Margio denied it and insisted he had nothing to do with Maharani's leaving, that she was not a little girl and it was up to her when to go and when to stay. As he said all this, Laila took note of his dejected, pitiable expression. She said no more, and like all the others, had no idea Margio would kill her father.

All of a sudden Margio told Agung Yuda, a village bully and friend: "I have a shameful idea."

He didn't explain what that shameful idea was and instead took Agung Yuda to Agus Sofyan's drink stall at one corner of the soccer field. He said he had some money and wanted a glass of beer. The stall had once been the lunch canteen for plantation employees and villagers, offering soups and small dishes to wives who were too lazy to cook. But since it was isolated, it became a hangout for toughs. Hidden by the rim of the cacao plantation, Agus

22

Sofyan started selling beer and arak. Sometimes weed and white sleeping pills were sold more discreetly, making the place a spot for getting drunk and making out—a daytime version of the nightwatch hut.

The Widow Laila came here often, becoming a target for the wild boys who would pester and try to grope her. Usually she would just giggle, but other times, if she felt generous, she would willingly go to bed with one of them for free. Some women might agree to be taken into the plantation to be fucked there, but not Laila. It was at that stall, while Laila was still watching the pigeon-racing, that Margio asked Agus Sofyan for a bottle of cold beer, which meant that Agus Sofyan would have to stick the bottle between blocks of ice rather than serve it chilled with little ice-chips. Margio always said it tasted different, and he was totally against forcing himself to sip a tepid beer. He and Agung Yuda shared that bottle of beer. Margio poured it into two glasses, sat on a small bench behind the stall and, while the beer was still fizzing, started talking again.

"Right now, I'm afraid I'm really going to kill someone."

Some time before his disappearance, Agung Yuda had heard Margio say he intended to kill his father. He had confessed there was something inside him, and that he could kill without hesitation. Agung Yuda had never asked what this something was, because he thought that even without it a boar herder could easily kill anyone. But of course nobody who hadn't been there would believe these words came from Margio. He was the sweetest and the most polite of his peers. Everyone knew his father was abusive, especially to his mother. And they knew how much Margio loved her. But the boy would typically give in to his father's brutality, damping down the old man's aggression, just as he restrained his friends when they started quarreling.

Even if he had been serious about killing his father, the opportunity had passed. Komar bin Syueb was six feet under. The odds of him coming back to life were slim, about on a par with the chances of Margio making an enemy, and so there wasn't a potential victim in sight. While some of his friends got into fights, he wouldn't lay a finger on anyone.

They spoke no more, because Agung Yuda didn't reply to Margio's confession. They just sat and sipped their drinks, peering into the cacao plantation crisscrossed by paddy fields, ponds, and peanut gardens. Over there, darkness had arrived and clouds of mosquitoes had taken charge, but it was still bright by the marshland where people tending their ponds were still visible. Margio also saw Kyai Jahro clutching cassava and papaya leaves, and a cement sack filled with bran. His father had once cultivated rice there, too, but lacking agricultural skills, he'd neglected it. All that was left were groves of cassava that needed no tending, the leaves falling when the sheep that wandered there in herds rammed the plants. Margio never had any intention of taking over that plot of land.

The area around a grand colonial building at one side of the soccer field had become Margio's hangout. Whenever he and his friends skipped a boring class they came here. They would hide between the cacao trees and smoke cigarettes, one time mixing the tobacco with thorn-apple seeds to get high. They read Enny Arrow's mimeographed pornographic novels or the sexcapades of Nick Carter. Dime novels and comic books were banned at school, and no one dared to talk at their desks about comics like *The Blind Man from the Haunted Cave* or the one called *Panji the Skull*, about a hero who carried his lover's coffin everywhere he went. They could read these only in the cacao plantation.

At other times it would become a place for fighting and for making out, and once in a while local thugs killed each other there. Their common enemies were the plantation's foremen, who always accused the kids of stealing cacao and coconuts, which in truth they sometimes did. The foremen would chase them off the land on their bicycles. If anyone got caught, he would be dragged by the ear and handed over to the strict physical education teacher. Sometimes the plantation changed its function at night, when people with no toilet at home would take a dump there. Margio kept looking at the place, as if seeing the worst of his past.

Agung Yuda was one of those who witnessed how exceedingly happy the young man was when he came home to find his father dead. He thought that with Komar bin Syueb's death all the problems in the household would end. Now he realized that was nonsense. Agung Yuda thought Margio was feeling down, and all his rambling about a shameful idea and killing somebody was rubbish. Margio simply said what he did because he couldn't think of anything better to say.

"Laksamana Raja di Di Laut," a *dangdut* song, was playing on Agus Sofyan's dual-band radio, hanging near the door of the stall, an asset that, cranked up to full volume, enlivened every morning, afternoon, and evening. The radio was an old Panasonic, designed to run on batteries, wired up clumsily to the electrics. A customer had once used the top of the case as a fan and never remembered to return it, and the insides hung out in a messy tangle. But the half-dead machine could make enough noise to be heard booming at half the soccer field's

25

distance and, on certain days, people would huddle near it to listen to the league soccer games. The rest of the time it was tuned to a station devoted to *dangdut* and other types of pop music. The din added to the yells of those gambling on the pigeon races as they tried to urge the birds onward.

Agung Yuda took from his pocket a half-full pack of Marlboros and gave one to Margio, who rolled it around between his fingers without lighting it. He was good at this, having mastered the trick using a ballpoint pen whenever he felt bored at school. Some friends copied him, giving the trick a try with a lit cigarette. Margio emptied his beer then stood up to leave.

"I forgot that I had to see Anwar Sadat," he said, without saying why.

He lit the cigarette before leaving. Agung Yuda still had no notion that Margio was going to kill Anwar Sadat. He watched Margio walk away, his tentative steps making it clear he wasn't sure whether to go or stay with Agung Yuda on the bench. But after looking back for a moment at his buddy, he headed off, the cigarette clasped between his lips. The cigarette crackled, glowing bright in the late-afternoon breeze, wisps of smoke rising around his head.

Twenty minutes later Agung Yuda regretted letting him go. He was still slumped on the bench, thinking that he had no problem with Anwar Sadat, so had no urge to follow Margio. His beer still filled half the glass. It had become their habit to savor every sip, making one glass last through hours of conversation. But with Margio gone, Agung Yuda might as well drain his glass. A few drops trickled down his chin, and he wiped them off with the hem of his shirt and tossed the cigarette to the ground, crushing it under his sandal.

Inside the stall sat a coy woman who flirted with him. Agung Yuda put his arm around her shoulders and the woman laughed, until his hand slipped into her bra and squeezed.

The woman wriggled and cursed, brushing him off, but Agung Yuda was laughing when he left her. He pissed against an electricity pole, then headed for the soccer field, and all the while, unknown to him, the hour drew closer when Margio would kill Anwar Sadat.

At that precise moment, Anwar Sadat was feeding his tame turkeys with a plate of leftover rice from the kitchen, fattening them up in the hope he could butcher them for the Lebaran holiday. Nearby, Ma Soma was sweeping the surau's yard, meaning Anwar Sadat's yard, cleaning away the fallen, yellow starfruit leaves and the rotten, maggot-ridden fruits, squishy from the heavy rain. They didn't exchange words, but acknowledged each other imperceptibly. Ma Soma finally left to clean the surau's water tubs of moss and ferns, and Anwar Sadat went into his kitchen to return the dirty plate.

He was the only one home apart from Maesa Dewi, who lay curled up on her bed, keeping her little boy company during his afternoon nap. This woman hadn't done much since her return with the newborn and her then future husband. Mostly she just lay in bed with her baby and finished up the cooked rice from the kitchen cupboard. Kasia had kicked the husband out to find a job, so he'd become the manager of a nearly bankrupt cinema away from the village, and returned just once a month with some money that Maesa Dewi would use up in a week. Kasia didn't care to think about them much, and Anwar Sadat couldn't really help as long as their primary finances lay in Kasia's grip, so he let the woman and child become parasites, just like Laila.

27

Anwar Sadat didn't see the boy wandering about in the yard, looking wildly nervous and pale. Then Margio stood leaning against the starfruit tree, staring into the house, catching glimpses of the man. It wasn't like anyone would have thought Margio really intended to kill him. Several people at the soccer field saw him, and Ma Soma, who came to throw a wastebasket full of moss and ferns into the garbage pit, spotted him and saw that he was unarmed. No one could have suspected Margio was about to commit murder, because for that he would have to be carrying a knife or a cleaver or a rope. Who could predict he might end a man's life with a bite? When Ma Soma passed by yet again, they still didn't speak. Margio was just languidly kicking at the tire swing, and appeared at one moment to be on the verge of leaving the yard. But he stayed there, like a thief looking for an opening, feeling he might be watched in turn. The people at the soccer field saw him for sure, but they knew Margio too well to be suspicious. No one gave a damn, and it seemed that Ma Soma wouldn't pop up again, as he was pumping well water to fill up the surau's tubs. The front door was now open, and it looked like Anwar Sadat was about to get some fresh air. Margio started to move.

At nearly ten past four, Anwar Sadat was leaving the house to look for someone to talk to at the soccer field. Just as he got no pleasure from watching cockfights, he was not much into pigeons either, though he would watch a race once in a while and place a bet just to be sociable. He was still wearing the shorts and the ABC jewelry store undershirt he had worn at the pancake stall that morning, and would die in that same attire. As soon as he noticed Margio walking toward him, Anwar Sadat froze, never making it past the door, as he waited for the boy, feeling that something was up. He was thinking of Maharani. Like Laila, Anwar Sadat knew the girl had been with this kid the previous night at the herbal tonic company's film screening. Anwar Sadat was hoping to find out why she had left so suddenly. He waited until Margio walked in and stood before him, but he didn't say a word about Maharani. His face was still pale and his lips quivered, as though it was Anwar Sadat who was going to dish out trouble.

As Margio later confessed to the police, yes, he killed the man by biting through an artery in his neck. There was no other weapon available, he said. He had thought about hitting him, knowing for certain that Anwar Sadat had grown feeble and lacked the strength to fight back. But Margio doubted his fists could end the man's life. He didn't believe he could strangle him either. A chair would only break a few bones, and the noise would wake Maesa Dewi. He hadn't seen her, but knew she would be in her room, just as she was every day.

The idea came to him all of a sudden, as a burst of light in his brain. He spoke of hosting something inside his body, something other than guts and entrails. It poured out and steered him, encouraging him to kill. That thing was so strong, he told the police, he didn't need a weapon of any kind. He held Anwar Sadat tight. The man was startled and struggled, but the pressure holding his arms was intense. Margio yanked his head back by the hair and held it immobile. He sank his teeth into the left side of Anwar Sadat's neck, like a man roughly kissing the skin below his lover's ear, complete with grunts and passionate warmth. The victim was too confounded to make any sense of what was happening. Nevertheless, the piercing pain and the shock to his chest forced Anwar Sadat to squirm, kicking over a chair. The sound of it hitting the floor and Anwar Sadat's brief yelp woke Maesa Dewi, who got up and asked from her room, "Papa, what was that?"

Anwar Sadat could reply only with a dying yowl. Margio replied with one deadly bite, gnawing and ripping out a lump of flesh, making a gaping hole in the man's neck. Delicate veins and tendons hung from the torn flesh, and the blood spurted. The tasteless piece of meat rested in Margio's mouth until he abruptly spat it on the floor, where it squirmed here and there. Anwar Sadat began to fly, his throat making unearthly sounds, while Margio's face was painted with gushing blood.

"Papa, what was that?" Maesa Dewi asked again.

Anwar Sadat was fluttering his wings, carried away by unconsciousness. Margio still held him tight, keeping him from falling. As soon as he heard Maesa Dewi's high-pitched anxious voice, the rustle of a blanket, the creaking of a bed, and the sound of feet on the floor, Margio sank his teeth once more into the dark red wet hollow, a second kiss more lethal than the first, and driven by a vast desire. He clenched his jaws more tightly, tore off another lump of flesh, and spat it out. He kept at it, biting repeatedly, as though driven by an unfathomable hunger, making the hole deeper and messier, bubbles and waves of blood freely spattering the floor.

He nearly chewed off the head, gnawing at Anwar Sadat's neck until the trachea was visible, a flash of ivory before the flooding red. The bedroom door partly opened, and Maesa Dewi stood there in white satin pajamas with a peony motif and one cheek marked by lines left from the folds of her pillow. Her half-awake eyes quickly widened and her slender hand jerked up, fingers covering her open mouth, unable to make a sound.

The scene was forever burned into Maesa Dewi's retinas, there for years, unexpunged for decades, an image more brutal than any horror film. She saw the half-severed neck; even the throats of cows slaughtered for the Festival of Sacrifice never looked that ghastly. There were clods of flesh scattered all over the floor, like spilled spaghetti sauce. The white tiled floor with its streaks of red blood resembled the national flag. And still standing there was Margio, his face a mask of gore, nearly unrecognizable, while his hands and shirt were just as repulsive. For a moment they exchanged a glance at the strangest threshold of conscience, in a state where both comprehended the hideousness of what had happened.

Maesa Dewi registered a strange and pungent odor, like garlic, floating thick in the air in gray clouds, hovering around her tresses and tumbling around her shoulders, so intense that it made her light-headed. Other confused sensations came over her: a stale sour taste, the clamor of insects humming, a churning in her bowels. Maesa Dewi saw a bright but unrecognizable blur, radiating a glare that made her squint, pushing her back until her head knocked against the door, which propped her up for a moment before she sank to the floor. Her body slumped, not in the way of someone sleeping peacefully, but more like a princess swiftly turned to stone. She even forgot how to scream, and forgot where she was. All the bits and pieces of what had just happened created a racket that woke her child, who now sat up with a wide-open mouth, crying, peeing, calling his mother the only way he could. Maesa Dewi slept on, collapsed on the floor and without a blanket.

Margio loosened his grip, stepped away from Anwar Sadat, and found a handful of the man's hair slipping through his fingers. The body danced for a moment, without rhythm, before slithering and crashing to the floor. Margio looked at him, watching carefully, until he was certain the man was dead. Had the severing of his jugular not introduced Anwar Sadat to the Angel of Death, the crack of his head on the floor would have completed the formalities. There he lay, with his navel exposed under the ABC jewelry store undershirt, like a helpless old man after a vicious ajak attack. This is how Ma Soma and others would find him.

Margio was fascinated by his masterpiece, which was more thrilling to the soul than one of Raden Saleh's cheap reproductions that hung above the television set. A whirl-wind spun in his head. He couldn't remember the way to the door, and fumbled about as the world suddenly became dark. Like Anwar Sadat, he danced for a while, twisting about but never falling, before steering himself toward the rear of the sofa, leaving a trail of red footprints. Margio dragged himself out, crawling inch by inch, and collapsed on the side porch.

The taste in his mouth forced the memory of the carnage upon him, and his primal instinct told him to walk away. Margio got to his feet, not exactly upright, and stumbled toward the starfruit tree, where he spat out the last bit of Anwar Sadat's neck. He saw it hit the ground, the size of a piece of tofu, and the sight of it sent the entire contents of his stomach surging, assaulting his throat with a bitter, sour taste. Leaning against the tree, the boy vomited the noodles he had for breakfast. It was some time before the turmoil in

32

his bowels came to an end. He was still gagging though there was nothing left to throw up. He left the starfruit tree, guided by the loud noises of the gamblers and the whistles on the pigeons' tails.

That was when Ma Soma emerged from the surau and saw him lurching unsteadily, smeared with blood. Alarmed, he almost ran after him, but then froze at the trail of red foot-prints the length of the yard from the house. He saw the overflowing puddle on the doorstep, and his feet pushed him to go forward, where he caught sight of the corpse lying sol-emnly in wait. His mind was nothing but a void until a voice inside him whispered in explanation. He lifted Maesa Dewi onto the couch, and grabbed a batik cloth to cover Anwar Sadat's corpse. Someone else, at the side of the soccer field, saw Margio and shouted:

"My God, someone's beaten Margio to a pulp."

The hubbub stopped and heads turned. Margio walked toward them, bringing cars to a halt, making motorbikes skid to a halt. People stared at him as if he were a premature ghost, out in the daylight. The birds became still, and the children stopped playing. Time was bound to a stake. They circled him, keeping their distance, as if he were likely to explode. They were struck dumb until one of them, Agung Yuda, got hold of a single clear question.

"Who beat you up?"

Margio stood there, unresponsive and uncomprehending. He recognized the faces around him, and at the same time he didn't. Agung Yuda, whose dumb head couldn't wrap itself around the likeliest explanation, approached and sniffed him to make sure it was real blood and not wall paint. Once he had convinced himself this was a face no longer sweet or

33

polite, but tragic, he found a simple explanation, one he realized was actually smart when it dawned on him, and he blurted out an important declaration:

"He's not hurt." That was a fact.

The night tumbled upon them, buoying the stars and hanging up a severed moon. The lamps in the front yards and along the streets were coming on, and the flying foxes were no longer visible, for the darkness enveloped their black bodies. Joni Simbolon dragged Margio off to the subdistrict military headquarters. This always happened before a suspect was sent to the police station. It provided the soldiers with some much-needed fun in a republic no longer at war. They locked him up in a cell, put him in a black uniform that smelled of mothballs and wooden cupboards, and let him curl up on a mattress facing a cup of warm milk he did not drink and a plate of rice and tuna he did not touch.

Major Sadrah visited him after the funeral prayers to make sure they didn't mistreat him. Soldiers on duty were always itching to deal roughly with any captured prey. They still respected the old veteran and would listen to what he said. So he hurried down there, where people milled around the Siliwangi tiger statue and the flagpole, laughing. They turned to him expectantly, hoping for a still more amazing story.

"I arrested him to prevent any unnecessary act of vengeance," Joni Simbolon said.

"Nonsense, Anwar's three children are all women," said the old veteran.

But there were still relatives, and others who might not be happy about the brutality of what had taken place in their neighborhood. Sadrah told them to keep him locked up until dawn, when the police would come. He wondered how

Maharani would react if she came home tomorrow morning and found that her father was dead and the killer the boy who had taken her to the movies. The crime was cut and dried, but he was looked for the malevolent spirit behind it, for some secret motive no one yet understood. His wife, who accompanied him and had been among the mourning women, whispered something that had become common knowledge, that the girl was crazy about Margio. But Major Sadrah hadn't seen any sign of Anwar Sadat objecting.

His feet brought him to the cell. He stood by the door, watching Margio shiver on the mattress, hoping that the secret would be revealed with a simple question. But bitterness and pity weighed on him, preventing him from speaking, and as he struggled Margio turned to him and understood his unspoken question.

"It wasn't me," he said calmly and without guilt. "There is a tiger inside my body."

Two

The tiger was white as a swan, vicious as an ajak. Mameh saw it once, briefly, emerging from Margio's body like a shadow. She would never see it again. There was one sign that the tigress was still inside Margio, and Mameh didn't know if anyone else had spotted what it was. In the dark, the yellow glint of a cat's eye shone in Margio's pupils. At first, Mameh was scared to look into those eyes, terrified that the tiger might actually reemerge. But with time and frequent exposure to Margio, she grew used to seeing those eyes light up in the dark, and she stopped worrying. The tigress wasn't her enemy and wouldn't hurt her; maybe it was there to protect them all.

Margio himself chanced upon it one morning, waking up from a solitary sleep in the surau, weeks before he ran away. The tiger's dancing tail brushed his bare feet and disturbed him, and for a moment he thought it was Ma Soma patting him awake so they could perform Subuh prayers together. He opened his eyes to see not steaming coffee on a tray or a plate of fried rice, but a white tiger lying next to him, licking its paws. It was past daybreak. The sky presented to the world an endless wet grey countenance. It had plainly been raining hard all night, and no one had emerged to do the prayers. Naturally Margio was stunned. All he could do was stare in awe at the stout beast as it contentedly groomed itself.

He knew the beast wasn't really alive. In his twenty years on the planet, he had gone in and out of the jungle on the outskirts of town and never seen such a thing. There were boars, small clouded leopards, ajaks, but no white tigers nearly the size of a cow. It reminded him of his grandfather, who had passed away years ago. He teared up and slowly extended a hand, reaching for the tigress's front paw. It was really there, with fur as soft as a feather duster. Its retracted claws signaled friendship, and as the paw rose up, Margio's hand reached for it again, and the tigress gave him a playful, kittenish tap. Margio tried to grap the animal's paw, but it rolled away from him, and then crouched, set for attack. Before Margio could dodge, the tigress lunged, and the pair started wrestling. He was laying flat on his back, breathless, when the tiger backed off, sat down next to him, and resumed licking its paws. Softly Margio patted its shoulder.

"Grandpa?" he said.

His grandfather had lived in a village far away. Margio would take a motorcycle taxi to the edge of the jungle, where a row of small shops known as the Friday Market was a terminus for various vehicles that made the journey up the ascending dirt path. An ox cart might be able to push its way farther uphill, but motorcycles would have a hard time of it, and the taxi drivers were reluctant. To visit Grandpa, Margio had to trudge up the hill through albizia trees and clove woods, on paths lined by mahogany trees, deep into the wild jungle known only to hunters. It took an hour to cross a stretch of hill as familiar to Margio as it was to the boars who would one day become his quarry. Behind the hill was a hamlet, bordering a madrasa with rice fields and fishponds. His grandfather didn't live there, but it was a place where Margio could unwind. He had come to know several locals after passing through time and again, but he couldn't hang out for too long. He had to continue his journey before evening fell and the ferry service stopped. The ferry was a raft of bamboo poles, attached to a wire stretched across the river. The steersman stood by the prow, pulling on the wire, dragging the raft slowly to the other side. If the current rendered the raft unsteady, he would use a long pole. The river was deep and the current gentle. There were no crocodiles, but there was the River Spirit, a great rolling wave, never seen but greatly feared by children. The raft cost a mere ten pennies per crossing and could carry dozens of people, as well as cows and sheep and sacks of rice and other crops. Getting off the raft was not the end of Margio's journey. He had to go up another hill on a truly slippery path. From the summit he could see a wide expanse of paddy fields below. In the middle of the vastness was a hamlet, full of greenery and houses, like a desert oasis, with coconut trees almost touching the sky. This was where his grandfather lived.

Margio first made the journey on his own when he was eight. Afterward he took every opportunity to go there, to see Grandpa, despite the journey taking half a day. He always had a good time, and always would come home with a bunch of bananas or a basket of langsat and durian fruit, which would definitely make Mameh happy, as well as his mother and father. Sometimes, if he badly wanted to go but had no money for the motorcycle taxi, he would walk to the Friday

Market and keep walking until he arrived at Grandpa's house, happy despite the exertion. So often did he take the path that he changed his route at times, quickly making friends with the villagers and the genies who inhabited the jungle. Later, his fellow boar hunters would never have to worry about getting lost so long as he was with them.

Despite his head of silver hair, Grandpa was not crookbacked but fit and vital. He was healthy right up to the moment he passed away in his bed, leaving a contented-looking body to be found later in the hut. Every day he took care of a rice field and a plantation, until the whole lot vanished without a trace in a transaction made by Margio's father. Margio really loved his grandfather. The old man would take the boy to a rivulet he called the Kingdom of Genies. Never ever tease a girl genie, he always said, but if one of them falls in love with you, take her, for that is a blessing. His grandfather said that girl genies were very beautiful. Margio always wished that one day he would meet one and that she would fall in love with him, but that promise hung tauntingly in the future no matter how many times he visited the rivulet.

More astonishing than the genies was the story of Grandpa's tigress. According to Ma Muah, the village story-teller, many a man in the hamlet had a tigress of his own. Some married one, while others inherited a tigress, passed down through the generations. Grandpa had one from his father, which before had belonged to his father's father, and so on right on up to their distant ancestors. Nobody remembered who was the first to marry the tigress.

On warm nights, Ma Muah would tell tales on her porch. Children huddled around her legs, and the girls took turns to massage her shoulders. If she was spinning a yarn late in the afternoon, the girls checked her hair for lice. She was always ready with a new story. She didn't have to make anything up, she would say; they were all true. Like the tigresses, many stories were passed between successive storytellers across the generations. But some were about the present and understood only by the chosen ones, and of course Ma Muah was the chosen granny.

As far as Margio could remember, Ma Muah didn't have a husband or a child, and had no work to do either, other than endlessly reeling off stories. She could go to anyone's kitchen and eat there, or someone would come to her shack bringing food. People loved her, especially children. She had a story about a blind woman with snakes and scorpions in her hair instead of lice, and who ate only the tubers of the purple nut sedge. There was the story of genie princesses who abducted handsome young men and brought them to their realms. They were not malevolent so long as no one barged into their dwelling place. Margio had come to know these places, namely springs, river pools, the peaks of hills, large trees, and the minarets of mosques. Still, nothing appealed to Margio's curiosity more than the protective white tigresses.

According to Ma Muah, the tigresses lived with their owners and guarded them against all dangers. She said that Grandpa was among those who kept a white tiger. But he would never talk to his grandson about the tiger because, he said, Margio was too young and couldn't possibly tame such a savage animal. It was bigger than a clouded leopard, bigger than the ones people saw at the zoo or circus or in schoolbooks. If a man couldn't control his beast, it could turn so violent that nothing could restrain it once enraged.

41

"But I just want to see it," said Margio.

"Later! Maybe then you will own it."

He had often heard of his grandfather's prowess, and that of elders in other hamlets: how they resisted Dutch efforts to abduct the best young men for forced labor in the Land of Deli. Bullets had no effect on them, nor did the samurai swords of the Japanese, who came later, and if they got angry, their white tigresses came out from their bodies to attack. They even expelled the gangs of Darul Islam guerrillas roaming the jungle. Ma Muah said that this was all because of the elders' elemental friendship with the tigresses, who became family through wedlock.

It was never clear to Margio what such marriages meant. He couldn't imagine a man sitting on a wedding dais beside a tigress wearing tassels on her head, powder on her befurred cheeks, and lipstick on her mouth, while the master of ceremonies prayed that the marriage of Mr. So-and-so to this tigress be blessed by the Almighty. As a teenager, he thought it would be very strange for a man to have sex with his tiger wife, and wondered what kind of children such a union would produce. Ma Muah would show off her toothless gums in laughter, chuckling every time he told her about his notion of the marriage between a human and a tiger.

"Only men marry tigers," Ma Muah said, "but not all the tigers are female."

His grandfather of course had a wife, a human woman, and clearly that made the tigress a kind of co-wife. Grandpa never married the tigress, because he inherited her from his father, but still for the family she was another spouse, loved and revered, sometimes more so than the human wife. Grandma was the first to die, succumbing to the pitiless onslaught of tuberculosis. The disease ruined their nights with nonstop coughing and an interminable fever as her body shrank toward the grave. His grandfather never remarried. Maybe the tiger wife was enough, although he didn't live much longer, too grief-stricken by Grandma's departure.

One evening, on Margio's last visit before his grandfather's death, the old man said firmly: "The tiger is white as a swan."

He wanted Margio to recognize the tigress if she came to him. Grandpa added that if the beast wished it, she might go to Margio's father and become his. Margio would then have to wait until his father died to take possession of the tigress. But if she didn't like his father she would someday come to Margio, and she would be his.

"And if she doesn't like me?" Margio asked anxiously.

"She will go to your son, or your grandson, or she might never reappear if our family forgets her."

The tigress had come to him, lying beside him on the surau's warm rug, while the universe outside froze. As his grandfather had said, the tigress was white as a swan or a cloud or cotton wool. How unbelievably happy he was, for the tigress was more than anything he had ever owned. He thought about how she would hunt with him, helping to corral the wild pigs that ruined the rice fields, and, if he ever got slack when one or two boars charged, she would protect him from the worst. It had never occurred to Margio that the tigress would turn up on such a damn cold morning, surrendering herself to him like a girl. Look how the tigress lay down, still licking the tips of her paws, tongue flickering. For a moment she seemed like a giant domestic cat, grandly aristocratic and huge. Margio looked deep into her face, so lovely to him, and the boy fell profoundly in love.

He wrapped his arm around her neck, embracing her and feeling the warmth of her fur against his body. It was like sharing an embrace with a girl on a cold morning, stark naked in bed, the most tender intimacy after a night of love-making. Margio closed his eyes, ecastatic after his long wait, free from yearning, reassuring himself that the tales he'd heard as a child were all true. But of a sudden he felt an abrupt pang of loss. The beloved had left without a word and warmth vanished with her. Margio opened his eyes, and saw that the animal had gone.

He was more surprised now than when he first saw her. The boy stood up and searched, but the surau was small, and he could soon tell that not a trace of her was left. Not even one scrap of fur. The rain still fell hard enough to make children on their way to school outside complain. In downpours such as this banana leaves would be cut from the trees, becoming disposable umbrellas, but Margio was not thinking about any of that. He thought of nothing other than his tiger. Standing still, he opened his mouth to call but not a sound emerged. He didn't know what to call the tiger. Grandpa never told him her name; neither did Ma Muah. Maybe he was supposed to name her himself, but there was little point in that when the animal was nowhere to be found.

He might have had his heart broken eleven times over by girls he loved dearly, and still the pain he felt now would surpass all of those rejections rolled into one. He struggled not to weep. No, it wasn't a dream, he said to himself. She had come to him because she was his. He had felt the softness of her fur, and they had played together. It was too real to be a morning's silent dream. Having searched and searched, and feeling sure that she had gone, his heartache grew into resentment. He shivered and his fingers clenched. Never had he felt so ruthless and vengeful a rage, and he couldn't evade it; he had to bear the pain. She had made him fall in love, the climax to years of longing, and he would not be deserted in this way.

He pounded on the door, scratched it, until the dark green paint peeled off its mahogany planks, and out of his mouth came a heavy growl that shattered the air. The deep scratches shocked him. Margio stood still and silent while his anger abated. He stared at the three parallel scratches, blistering wounds had they been on someone's back, then checked his hands. His fingernails weren't long. He kept them short so they wouldn't be a nuisance when he held his spear for pig hunting. His nails couldn't have etched marks like these into the door. Still, he saw paint and timber flakes under his short fingernails. For some time Margio was frozen in awe and puzzlement, until he understood what must have happened. She hadn't left him. The tigress was there, a part of him, the two of them inseparable until death. He leaned against the wall, rubbed his navel, below which he sensed the tigress now resided. She wasn't tame after all.

To Agung Yuda, he jokingly said: "I'm not single anymore."

Agung Yuda thought he meant he was no longer a virgin, which wasn't earth-shaking news and he didn't pay much attention. He assumed Margio wanted to brag about sleeping with that Maharani girl. Who else could it be? He had seen them together during her vacation. And so no one found out there was a tiger inside his body, other than Mameh, who had caught a glimpse of it that one time, until Margio himself confessed shortly after killing Anwar Sadat.

On the night before Margio met his tiger, he had told his sister Mameh for the first time that he wanted to kill their father. Mameh had already heard this from someone else. Margio had been cursing their old man over and again at the nightwatch post, and similar sentiments had been heard elsewhere—that if the chance arose he would kill Komar bin Syueb. But nothing happened, and there was no sign that it would. It was just the rage of a boy resentful of his father. And such anger fades with time. So when Margio made the same boast to Mameh, the girl too ignored him; or perhaps she secretly hoped he would do it.

Back then she hadn't yet caught the feline glint in Margio's eyes, but she could sense the fury rising like heat into the crown of his head. The feeling became more intense over the days that followed, after their week-old baby sister, Marian, died. Mameh kept knives and machetes away from Margio, and kept a constant eye on him. She honestly didn't care if he actually killed their father, but every corner of Mameh's remaining sanity drove her to curb any such foolish intentions.

Incensed at the realization that he couldn't make good on his threat, Margio left home. At the time, there were tents lit up on the soccer field, girls selling tickets, the trumpeting of elephants, tigers roaring. When the Holiday Circus came to their neighborhood, it put on shows for two weeks. No one could predict its arrival, and it might be a year, two or even five, as once happened, before it reappeared. But its very presence was a great treat for the townsfolk, no matter how familiar the attractions had become. Not much changed over the years, except that the young women they called "plastic girls" were replaced by pinker and younger entertainers.

He went on his own, quietly bought a ticket, his hands thrust into the pockets of a dirty pair of jeans. He hadn't seen a circus in a long time, not since his father took him way back when he was a little boy, but this time he was impelled not by a desire to see something spectacular, but by a need to sink himself into a river of people, to lose himself in the noise, and to hide. He took a seat on the highest tier, almost touching the ceiling, and sat chin in hand waiting for the show to start.

His mind was a blank when the black-jacketed circus manager in a crisp bow tie welcomed them with a fixed smile, delivering a short speech that summed up the circus's journey across the archipelago. He described a ship where they performed on Navy Day, and rattled out plans for future performances. Even when a beautiful woman in a top hat decorated with peacock feathers, sporting a bright red waistcoat, black stockings, shiny red shoes and a matching miniskirt that revealed her underwear, read out the order of attractions through tantalizing crimson lips, Margio held fast to his meditation, free from the smutty thoughts that usually came to him when he saw a beautiful and provocatively dressed woman.

Squinting slightly, he propped his chin on his fist, sandwiched on one side by a fat woman and her small child, both eating peanuts and drowning out the music with their chomping, and on the other by an uncomfortable young man whose girlfriend kept squirming against him, pestering him for a hug. Perhaps he was wary of Margio, who fumed silently, his body language deterring all approach.

Margio had hoped to forget the anger he had brought here from home. He wanted to watch the plastic girls and could think of nothing more captivating than these lithe

47

young women, their lovely legs entwined on a round rotating table or dangling from intertwining ropes. He closed his eyes so as not to see the orang-utan tracing circles on a tiny motorcycle. When it stopped, he knew its trainer would glumly have to push the bike along. Nor did Margio want to see a parrot on a bicycle, a sight that raised a clamor of applause from the children. The clowns annoyed him, too, making him wish he could make them disappear with a snap of his fingers. Even when the female acrobats, the plastic girls, came out and jumped on one another to form a human pyramid, which soon crumbled in the most graceful manner imaginable, he felt cold. The spectacle didn't touch him in the least.

Margio was about to leave for Agus Sofyan's stall and a drink, when they brought out a flat iron frame. He knew what that meant. Rooted to the spot, he waited with a pounding heart. The circus crew worked quickly and carefully, and soon a magnificent twenty-foot-tall cage was ready, and Margio heard the roar of a beast that made his blood surge and his heart race even faster. He was no longer propping up his chin. His hands fell onto his knees, and sweat soaked his shirt. He waited very patiently, watching the cage door being attached to the rear of a truck, while an animal tamer stood by in his sparkling silver costume, his forbidding whip uncoiled. Then the truck door opened and reluctantly the graceful beast walked toward the cage, every now and then turning back to the truck, until the tamer forced it forward, lashing the floor menacingly, and the tiger, looking bored, jumped to the center of the cage.

Nostalgia overwhelmed him, dragging back old memories as he watched the striped body ascend and sit on a tall, round

48

wooden stool. There it squatted and scratched its nose. To be exact, it was licking its paw, and using the wet paw to wash its face. Perhaps it had just woken up, or was primping itself for the benefit of the ladies and gentlemen of the audience. Before long, out came its mate, along with a pair of Indian lions. The tigers were not a swan-like white, but brown, like old sepia-toned photographs. But despite this and not being as large as a cow, they lacked nothing in grandeur. Margio felt a kinship with them, moved by the unexpected sight, as if fate was guiding events and all he had to do was keep moving.

Long after Grandpa's death, he would while away the days waiting for his white tiger. He began to suspect it had become his father's property. This was probably what made him wary of Komar bin Syueb, keeping a cautious eye on him in case some telltale sign gave away the tiger's presence. In all those years, he never saw any hint that it was there, although there was nothing to suggest the contrary either. Throughout those rage-filled months, he burned with an uncontrollable jealousy. Like a genie, Margio watched Komar bin Syueb invisibly, from near and far, to see if he ever communicated with the animal. Eventually, he tired of the exertion. Margio grew reconciled to the idea that it was either Komar bin Syueb's or it would never belong to him or his son.

The night at the circus changed that. When the show ended and he was jostling his way through the crowd, his hands in his pockets again, his mind was filled with pictures of untamed bodies. He couldn't shake off what he had seen, and when he saw the painting of a tiger on the tent's canvas wall, it drove him wild with longing, like the sight of an alluring woman. Under a spotlight, and close to the humming diesel engine by the box office, Margio leaned against the fence and was almost back inside, eager for another date with the tiger couple, when he realized he didn't have the money for a second ticket. He walked along the circus fence, hoping to catch sight of the caged animals in the middle of the soccer field, but the crew seemed to have locked them away securely. His blood was hot, and he thought that perhaps Grandpa's tiger was already inside him. What was needed was a way to bring it out.

That night he didn't go home. He wanted to be alone with the tigers in his head. He went to the surau close to midnight and lay there, seeing tigers on the ceiling, in the imam's niche, under the drum stand—everywhere. Since he was a little boy he had been sleeping in the surau or at the night-watch post, possibly spending more time in these places than at his own home. That night he dreamt about a genie princess emerging from a spring, asking him to marry her, and the princess looked like Maharani. When he woke up the next morning, a white tiger lay beside him. That was how it began.

Margio himself could never explain why he was so angry with Komar bin Syueb. To him it was like a debt that he needed to collect. The debt had grown over time until it weighed painfully upon him. Perhaps the only thing that prevented his rage boiling over into violence was his immeasurable love for his mother and sister. Komar was their pillar, no matter how rotten and unsteady that pillar might be, however skewed it was. Margio wanted to finish him off, and he thought the day would come eventually, it was simply a matter of time, but it never happened. Throughout his life, he suffered most from suppressing his yearnings, hoping like a typical villager that everything would simply get better without his needing to do a thing, and reminding himself that the method he wanted to use could only lead to disaster.

He always likened himself to the demigod Kresna, who at the height of his merciless rage could turn into the giant Brahala, with his thousand heads, thousand hands, and immeasurable fury. No one could stop him, not even the gods. The great praiseworthy thing about Kresna, the King—for that was what Margio called him—was that only once in a while, and only briefly, did he let the monster out. Later on, Margio would think there was something inside of him that wanted to get out when his rage began to smolder, and his job was to restrain it, to keep it inside, because everything that happens has already been written down in the stories of the gods. No matter how great his anger, he had to suffer it, just as Kresna did before him.

For years, he was able to contain himself. He was a model of restraint until the night his little sister Marian died. Then he lost control and told Mameh that he wanted to kill Komar bin Syueb. For him, Marian's death was the greatest tragedy imaginable in their household, and he no longer wanted to suppress his brutal rage, a rage that he had often released on the rumps of boars during hunting season. Every time he goaded a boar with his spear, piercing it just enough to make the animal fear for its life, he thought of Komar bin Syueb beneath the spearpoint. Now he wanted to impale the old man for real and he couldn't keep it to himself; he had to vent his anger somehow and he did it in words, talking to Mameh.

Marian died a week before the circus tent went up in the

village. A scrawny newborn lacking milk, she spent her short life half-dead. She didn't have a fever, but was clearly about to die. Death swarmed around her like flies over a carcass, and everyone understood what was happening. They could see it in her eyes. Every time Margio looked at her, his grief was compounded by the sorrow in his mother's face. Komar seemed to be the only one who didn't care. He looked at the baby as if she were dirt, and people swore he never touched her. There were no playful games of peek-a-boo between this man and his daughter. The day came when Komar was supposed to shave her head, arrange a small ritual feast to assure her good luck, and of course give her a beautiful name, but he did no such thing.

Margio himself slaughtered Komar's fowl, without asking for permission, and joined a small ritual feast with Mameh and their mother. He grabbed his father's shaving equipment, cursing the old barber, while the baby, who couldn't cry, lay crumpled on its mother's lap. As for a name, Komar didn't make any suggestions. He chose to disappear, and their mother eventually proffered a single name—with no middle or family name attached.

"Marian."

When the end came, there was one source of comfort: the girl died with a name and with her head shaved. Margio managed to carve the name on her tiny tombstone, which stood under a frangipani tree that Mameh planted, where the aroma of ylang-ylang petals lingered. The baby's death fired Margio's hatred for his father; he thought that if he were ever to kill Komar, now was the time.

Komar bin Syueb came home just before dawn, not long after Marian's burial, neither guilt nor surliness evident in his

52

face. He might have slept at the brothel or the garbage dump; no one cared. No one greeted him, neither his family nor the neighbors. He was a half-dead, senile old man with no control over himself, entering the house without thinking to ask why everyone was sad. Yet he must have been aware of Marian's death, for it was the ritual meal that brought him home. He sat in the kitchen and shamelessly ate the leftover chicken, and then went to sleep, snoring horribly. Eventually Margio couldn't stand it any more. He snatched up a pan, the only pan they had, and slammed it on the floor, waking Komar with a great explosive crash.

With this action, the truce they had maintained for so many years came to an end. Komar understood that the boy had reached the limit of his patience. After that, the old man withdrew into his shell, spending long hours stock-still in bed, pretending to be oblivious to everything. It was the first time Margio had let out his anger—he had never dared before—and now his father understood what a furious cobra his son kept in his belly. Actually, Margio was as surprised as anyone by his outburst, which had set everything in motion; he had to ready himself. He was twenty, and he had absolutely nothing to fear from his fifty-year-old father. The old man, perpetually in bed, understood the limits age had set, grasping with a melancholy resignation the fact that Margio was no longer a young boy, but a man, against whom he had no means of defense.

In the days that followed, they kept their distance, preparing for battle and at the same time evading it. Komar bin Syueb was now so feeble and abstracted that Margio, seeing his father's helplessness, willed himself not to act too soon, holding his hatred in check, though it boiled white-hot right up until the morning he met his white tiger. His Brahala.

Mameh saw the tigress briefly, slipping out of Margio as easily as the boy might slip out of a shirt and pants. She recoiled, convinced the beast would pounce, and couldn't move for fear until it returned to its lair, deep inside Margio's chest. That was the evening when Margio came home to find their father slaughtering chickens. Komar asked no one for help, but clamped their feet and wings with his sandals, one hand gripping the poor chicken's head, the other swinging the kitchen knife. Slash, slash, he cut off their heads one by one, and threw the remains into the cage, their wings flapping to hold off the clutch of death.

"What's he up to?" Margio asked Mameh, without Komar hearing.

"He's planning a ceremonial meal for Marian's seventh day."

Perhaps it was this that drove the tiger out into the open. Margio could not tolerate the damned old man doing anything nice for the dead girl, whom he had completely ignored while she was alive. Margio had come to believe that Komar had killed his youngest, or had at least intentionally let her die. And now the accursed Komar was planning to arrange a seventh-day ceremony. Rot in hell, Margio thought, sure the baby's soul would accept nothing from this man. That was when Mameh caught sight of a reddish, spectral face, apparently covered in fur, a yellowish glint in its eyes. She heard an echoing roar and saw a white shadow dance in its pupils. She almost screamed before it disappeared again, settled behind a cage door that seemed to be shut tight. Margio had confined it, suppressed its savagery.

After the episode with the pan, Komar incarcerated himself in his bedroom, went out only to go to his

54

barbershop, and returned to nestle in bed. Those were the moments when he thought Margio would attack, if not actually kill him. The boy had suddenly grown terrifying. Komar found himself weighing up his son's statistics, his present age, height, weight, as if Margio were a prize-fighter, and worst of all was the possibility that he had inherited that damned tiger. The old man was wise enough not to worsen the friction between them. Margio was no longer the meek and submissive lad, sitting quietly in a corner of the house or leaving without a word. He could handle himself, and Komar bin Syueb knew better than to test those young muscles.

Later, Mameh saw her father leave his room, looking sweet as pie. No longer his old talkative self, Komar addressed himself to the chores he had often neglected. He took the palm leaf broom and began sweeping the floor, over and over, even though it was clean, and in the morning and after-noon he filled up the tub for them to wash. The next day, Mameh lost more of her regular tasks as, out of the blue, he deigned to wash their clothes. Mameh wanted to stop all this sweetness, annoyed that her father should have any energy left after his stint at the barbershop. He should have been tired out on his return, but he didn't seem to care. He ignored Mameh and left her with almost nothing to do.

She came to understand his intentions when she noticed the man himself slaughtering the chickens for Marian's seventh-day ritual. She only had to look at him to grasp the truth, as if a certain fate were written on his forehead. He was trying in vain to make peace with them, to erase the rancid traces that went a long way back. It was a vain effort. No one was moved by this overflow of questionable kindness. It was sad, too, because everybody felt it was too late for him to start again.

Margio was the least forgiving. His father's meekness was fuel to his son's hatred, which burned brighter than ever the minute the old man's intentions became clear. Don't think I'll forgive you, Margio thought. He left the house, unwilling to help with whatever Komar was doing, and wandered around various places, kicking the walls of the nightwatch post, drinking at Agus Sofyan's stall, or hurling coconuts in the abandoned plantation, while his father cleaned the chickens by himself, plucking their feathers, carrying the bodies to the kitchen, boiling and frying them, and cooking rice as well. Before dusk he visited the neighbors, inviting them to come after the Isha prayer, to gather together and read the Yassin, for the comfort of Marian's soul.

Margio returned after the neighbors had left, and the mats were still spread out. Up till then everything had been handled by Komar bin Syueb alone. Neither Mameh nor her mother had lifted a finger. Komar told Margio to eat—there was fried chicken and rice and potato stew—but Margio didn't want to touch it. He passed through the kitchen and went into his bedroom, came out again, went to the bathroom to piss and then stepped onto the terrace and stood under a lantern. Mameh came out to coax him to eat, but Margio's only response was to light a cigarette.

In the dim light, Mameh saw the increasingly luminous sheen and the yellow glint in his eyes. She still remembered how Margio had wanted to kill Komar. His eyes shone brilliantly with sharp, piercing rays, and Mameh thought that his stare alone could kill Komar bin Syueb. But she could see the boy's suffering, too. Sweet Margio was at war with evil

Margio, and it wouldn't end until his father's life was over. Mameh could see he was exhausted from fighting himself. But Komar bin Syueb would not die at Margio's hands or from the fangs of his pet tiger. That night, after flicking his cigarette butt into the yard, Margio said to Mameh, "I'm leaving" He added, "Otherwise I'll end up killing that man."

Mameh didn't take his words seriously. To her, he seemed to be saying, "I *want* to leave." In truth, he had gone long ago. These last few years, Margio had clearly grown unhappy at home, and his true permanent residence had become the nightwatch hut and the surau. He might not come back again to the family house, but he would still be found at his usual places. Mameh later saw how wrong she had been.

One day, on a morning like any other, they suddenly lost Margio. His friends were the first to realize he had gone. They hadn't seen him all day. Someone said he'd been at the circus, but that was its last night in the village, and the whole crew had packed up and left, and no one knew where they were heading. The entire village was certain that one of the circus girls had lured Margio into joining them. Everyone was sure he would return to his birthplace and his true love, who they felt confident was Anwar Sadat's daughter Maharani. Eventually, when some of his friends dropped by the house to ask after him, Mameh realized Margio really had run away.

His disappearance made a lot of people sad, particularly Major Sadrah, who was all set to kill some boars; and also Komar bin Syueb, it seemed. For a week he tried to ignore his eldest child's absence, returning to a familiar routine, feeding the remaining chickens and the three pairs of rabbits. Every morning Komar took out his old bicycle, worn thin with rust, its chain creaking, and like most bikes in the village without brakes or lights. Komar went to the market to gather rotten carrots and cabbages from the vegetable vendors' garbage, and returned home after stopping by the rice mill to get some bran. All this went to his animals. The bran had to be mixed with warm water, stirred and served in several coconut leaves to prevent the chickens from getting in each other's way, while the rotten cabbages and carrots would simply be thrown into the rabbit hutch. Komar busied himself, especially with his extra chores, to make it seem as if he didn't care about Margio's disappearance. But Mameh knew how he really felt.

One morning Komar asked, "Is Margio back yet?"

"Not yet," Mameh said quietly. "Believe me, he'll be back when it's time for him to get married."

This was no comfort to Komar, and soon his health declined with the onslaught of various illnesses. The sense of loss he felt was severe; he was back to spending whole days in bed, became dreadfully thin, and muttered in delirium. He gave up on cutting hair, and instead trimmed away at his own soul, snip by snip. Komar complained about a nail inside his stomach, later verified when he vomited blood. His skin turned blue and his body swelled. Mameh went to fetch a hospital orderly, who told her to drag him to the hospital. Mameh called on her mother's two younger brothers, who carried Komar on a stretcher. He had more diseases than the doctors had time to discuss, and was left to sleep in a cold and haunted ward.

His wife didn't want to take care of him in his final decline, and Mameh had to shoulder the burden. She could see the final moment was near. As the ylang-ylang rapidly blossomed, so did the champak, and ravens cawed in the distance.

After two days in the hospital, Komar asked to be taken home and said firmly to Mameh, "Don't call for any more doctors. I'm healthy enough to wait for my grave to be dug."

That was when Komar could still talk. A morning came when he couldn't open his mouth anymore. It shut in defiance of its master, his jaws unbelievably stiff. This had happened before, healing only after a long series of massages from a shaman who rubbed his neck and toes with onion juice. This time Mameh didn't know whether Komar would ever open his mouth again. Three shamans tried unsuccessfully to knead his jaws back to life. It was an all-too-obvious omen of his approaching death. Komar suffered greatly, rolled about on his mattress, smacked his cheeks, clawed at his mouth, adding his own tortures to the pains that wracked his body. He couldn't eat unless the food was turned to pulp. Mameh had to feed him vegetable gruel, which Komar would push in with his index finger, making himself cough, slobbering on his mattress. Soon his hands couldn't move either, as if the nerves had been cut. Mameh had to feed him sweet tea, as there wasn't much that Komar could eat. Within a few days his shrunken frame resembled a quivering house lizard.

One night Mameh heard Komar growl and, going to his side, asked if he was in pain. But it wasn't his body that tortured him and forced out a second grunt. He wanted to speak, so Mameh leaned close and strained to make out what he was saying. It was no good. Komar's mumbling was incomprehensible. Mameh cleverly thought of handing him some paper and a pencil from her schooldays, but that only increased his despair, because Komar's hands no longer functioned. Mameh came up with a better idea. She took the paper and pencil and every time she wrote something suitable, Komar would briefly nod and his mouth would strain to form a smile. It took half the night, and it felt like much longer, to put together a simple short sentence. In this way, the dying man managed to convey his last wish: "Bury me next to Marian."

The next day Mameh passed the message to her mother. For a long time, the woman had rarely opened her mouth, but to this wish she generously replied, "Tell that to the gravedigger."

Clearly, Komar bin Syueb had sought reconciliation at the end of his life, and in particular to make amends to the baby who had perhaps died because of him. Lying in bed at night, Mameh heard a crow make a rumpus on their roof. When it flew away, its cawing echoed in her memory. She wanted to ignore superstition, but everyone said that when a crow perched on a roof, it meant there would be a death in that house. She didn't fall asleep until dawn, and that was when he died, the pain and suffering of waiting for his eldest child's return too much for him. Nothing made Mameh sadder than the thought of her father longing for his son, even though she was pretty certain that had Margio come back before his father died, he would have taken Komar's life himself.

That morning, Mameh saw her father sprawled on his bed. His body had deteriorated into an anonymous lump of flesh, a sight to put even a crow off its food. No one had slit his throat, even though Komar had suspected that someday someone in their home would do it. Even Margio had refrained from cutting off his head. The old man died of natural causes, his mind gone. "Sayonara," he said, and slipped out through the grated window, towed along by the

Angel of Death, looking back at his final days, at his sour-smelling mattress, his damp bedroom, and his barren world.

That was the end of a long-established household routine. Just before daybreak, Mameh had been the first to wake up at number 131. As if sleepwalking, she would finish the tasks her half-dead father could no longer handle, she would go to his room with a small bucket containing warm water with a face cloth floating on top. In his final days, with the pain worsening rapidly, the smell of cemetery soil in his nostrils, Komar repented a little and forced his ailing body to pray. Mameh helped with the ablutions, washing his hands, feet, and face, and let him pray lying down. Five times a day. One touch from Mameh's hand was enough to wake him, telling him that the call to dawn prayer was imminent, and Komar would open his eyes, not moving at all, as if he was glued to his sheet, his head sinking onto three tiers of rotten pillows, his limp body obscured beneath the black and white striped blanket from the hospital.

When dawn came and the touch of Mameh's hand didn't awaken Komar, she shook him, but he didn't even twitch. His eyes were open, but he was gone. When she realized this, she swiftly put the bucket on the floor before she dropped it. The girl touched her breast, mumbled in bewilderment, and then, prompted by deaths she had seen in movies, she closed her father's eyes. "Sayonara," she said, your scissors and combs will testify for you. She looked around to make sure there was some exit from the room for his soul. Sat on the floor was a bowl containing the water she had used to cool Komar's forehead the previous night; elsewhere some vegetable gruel, an untouched green banana and a glass of fermenting sweet tea on the bedside table.

61

This was the daughter who in her entire eighteen years of life had never even been given a pair of earrings by her father. Hanging from her ears were coiled mattress threads, meant to prevent the pierced skin from sealing up. She had always been holding out for two or three grams of gold. True, Komar once took little Mameh out for a picnic by the sea, and proudly taught her how to make a sandcastle. True, Komar once told Mameh to go to a tailor to get herself a dress for Eid ul-Fitr. And one time he took her to the cinema to see *Pandawa Lima*. It was a safe bet that when he died, Mameh would remember none of those things, and the dead man knew it.

The muezzin's call floated in from the surau on the eastern side of Anwar Sadat's house. Following Ma Soma's husky voice came the sound of neighboring doors being opened, keys being turned or latches being slid into place, and the susurration of slippers dragging along the small alley to the surau, mongrels barking as they rose from a deep sleep, while roosters flapped their wings before crowing in four bursts of noise, the last one sounding like a long sigh. Mameh went to the room where she slept with her mother, and woke her to say: "Father's dead." When her mother got up she made sure her husband had died of natural causes, and not from being strangled by her daughter.

Afterwards, this woman Nuraeni just went to the kitchen and sat on a small stool facing the stove, mumbling to herself, to the stove and to the pan, which wasn't that unusual. She was a bit out of her mind, or at least that was how her daughter saw it. Mameh followed her to the kitchen, stood in the doorway, stared through the dimness, and waited. She had no idea what to do with her dead father. She hoped Margio would come back soon and bring them some direction, or else they might just let Komar bin Syueb rot in his bed.

In that stillness, Mameh heard a kind of sobbing, a soft whimper that seeped between her mother's meaningless mumbling. It shocked Mameh greatly to discover that this woman could miss the husband who spent his whole married life beating her up for this or that mistake or for no reason at all. Mameh was pretty well convinced that her mother was heartbroken not because she had loved Komar, but because she had grown used to a life with him, as tormenting as it was.

The animals Komar kept caged in the backyard were noisy, eager to be fed. Ever since Komar's decline began, there had been neither rotten vegetables nor bran for those poor creatures, and Mameh took over the task of caring for them, providing whatever leftovers she could find in the kitchen. Perhaps they might die now their master had left, she thought. But then again they might be sent after him sooner than that, should anyone wish to send him prayers in a ritual later that day. Mameh would be happy to cut off their heads, the way Margio had often secretly done.

The sobs from the kitchen droned on, and Mameh was still standing in the doorway, as if, at the end of a play's final act, she waited for the curtains to close on her. She wanted to distract her mother, to force her to do something, but she backed off, conceding that neither of them had any idea what was required. Mameh now turned on the kitchen lamp, whose switch was in the rice storeroom. It wasn't really a rice storeroom, more like a big boxroom containing a trunk in which papayas and bananas had been left to ripen, next to no more than two or three kilos of rice, which Komar would have bought from the market after

63

trimming people's hair. Under the bright beam, Nuraeni's whimpering paused, but she remained in an ecstasy of sadness, staring at the stove with her back to Mameh.

Trying to keep busy, thinking that things could probably go on as usual, Mameh took the pan which Nuraeni was communing with, and filled it full of water from the well. She lit the stove's wicks, and the creeping fire cast a light on her mother's puffy face, which suddenly looked as crumpled as a tiny doll's and paler than the corpse itself. As she put the water on the stove to boil, the way she had always done when she woke her father up at dawn, Mameh wondered if Komar bin Syueb's death could really be that painful for her mother. She herself was rather delighted.

They stayed silent a long time until she heard the voices of people returning from the surau. It crossed her mind to go outside, to greet them and announce that Komar bin Syueb was dead in the hope they would offer some help in dealing with the body, but she didn't know how to explain herself. It would be embarrassing and inappropriate to say, "Uncle, my father is dead," because the cheerful tone in her voice would betray her. She waited for the sound of footsteps to disappear, wishing Nuraeni would provide some advice, perhaps telling her to go to a particular house to deliver the news. When Marian died, Margio handled everything. Mameh didn't even know who to speak to.

Sounds of life multiplied, right and left, from the neighboring houses, as earthen and oil stoves were lit and children pissed on banana plants. Dirty dishes were stacked in the washbasins, water buckets were hoisted from the wells, and tubs were filled. She could hear bicycles passing by, rushing to the market carrying empty baskets, or full ones if the bicycle's owner was off to sell. Far along the street the bells of horse carts clanked in harmony with the clatter of iron horseshoes. Again the dogs barked, before rolling on the sandy ground to snooze once again. But in the kitchen there was only the sound of the simmering water and the soft rustle of Nuraeni's shaking shoulders. This is the woman Komar bin Syueb used to ride so cruelly, Mameh thought.

It was an incident long past, but Mameh would never forget what happened on a night so cold it brought on a frantic need to piss. She dammed up the urge until a flood threatened. Her bladder would be contained no longer and forced her out of bed. When she couldn't find her mother, she went to another room where Margio slept like a dead man. It was such a dark night that Mameh didn't have the courage to go to the bathroom alone, but the tranquility of Margio's sleep discouraged her from waking him up. Wondering where her parents were, Mameh crawled toward the kitchen, feeling around for the storeroom's light switch.

She didn't turn on the light. A neighbor's terrace lamp gleamed through the lattice window into the storeroom. Upon the trunk she saw two naked figures struggling with each other like the jockey and steed she had once seen at a Sunday horse race at the coconut plantation. As she stared at the silhouettes on the big trunk, images from that race flashed vividly through her mind. Nuraeni was bent forward like a horse at the gallop, and Komar bin Syueb was thrusting into her from behind. She could see Komar's buttocks whipping savagely, and each thrust was followed by Nuraeni's moan, like a cow whose throat was being cut. That idea was vivid, too, since Mameh had herself seen a cow's throat slashed for the Festival of Sacrifice.

65

She nearly wet herself, standing there, watching the sweat-soaked figures and listening to the moans of her mother being violently penetrated. She crawled to the bathroom, spilled the contents of her bladder, and returned to her room without once wanting to peek again into the storeroom. She couldn't sleep afterward. Over the years, the memory lived on, producing sadness and disgust respectively at the sight of her mother and father.

Mameh was only fourteen then, an age when she was perturbed and fascinated by the changes in her body, and in particular by the flesh that, as she put it, talking to herself, "had suddenly poked out of my chest." She looked at her nipples and thought, half-proudly, "They're like bullets," somewhat annoyed by their inconspicuous shape. If her shirt exposed her breasts, however slightly, men probed her with their eyes unpleasantly. Every morning her chest size seemed to have expanded overnight, a thought that sometimes made her wonder if a separate woman wasn't starting to emerge from the teenage girl.

She was happiest with her body when shut away in the bathroom. There was a large mirror over the water tub, the remains of a cupboard a cat had knocked over and smashed. The mirror was a magic window into an alternate world. Half of Mameh's time in the bathroom was spent standing naked, admiring her own form and those growing breasts. Here she felt like a complete woman. She liked her new breasts, praised them, cupping them with her hands, measuring their growth from one shower to the next, and sometimes jiggling them, wondering what was inside. She was urged on by her admiration of the bold and curvaceous mature women seen on the neighborhood streets. She was smaller in size, but in front of the mirror she mimicked the movements of the bigger, older women.

But the world accessed through that mirror was a vulnerable one, because the bathroom door no longer had a latch. Everyone thought to buy one when they took a shower, but no sooner were they dry than the idea was gone. Noise was the only sign that the room was occupied, and once, when Mameh had not touched the bathwater for minutes as she stood examining her new figure, the door was abruptly flung open. Time stopped.

Komar bin Syueb stood there in briefs and an undershirt, a cigarette in his mouth, hands holding the briefs' string to prevent them from slipping. Mameh screamed, floating and drifting a moment in consciousness, before collapsing and burying her face between her knees. Mameh would always recall the incident as taking a long time, lasting longer than her own life. Without lifting her face, Mameh heard Komar shut the door and slowly walk away without a word, feet wide as he struggled to restrain his need to shit. The moment he was gone, Mameh pissed herself.

Father knows my breasts stick out and there's a bush between my legs, she thought. He had uncovered his daughter's secrets. Throughout the years, Komar knew Mameh wished he could forget what had happened. Komar never did, though no one can say why. And Mameh knew as much. At first she avoided him whenever possible, and Komar had to leave her pocket money on the table. He had never wanted to see his daughter naked, and didn't now, despite the demonic nature that could possess him. But Mameh felt violated, and he could tell she did and prepared himself for the day when she came at him with a kitchen

67

knife. But like Margio, she demurred. Instead she nursed him as he died.

Komar's death was a happy event for Mameh. That same sense of happiness should have come to Nuraeni. Or was her sobbing a way of celebrating, a form of release?

Morning had come, and neither woman had done a thing with the body, which was stiffening on its bed. They remained imprisoned in the kitchen, moving around from time to time to ease their aching joints. The water had come to a boil with a whistle, and Mameh turned it off. She should be cooking rice, but the urge to get busy wilted at the sight of Nuraeni still ensconced on the stool in front of the stove.

Outside, schoolchildren had already passed by and the world had become warm and full of song. Only inside the house did the murkiness increase, with the closed doors, the scruffiness of the two women, their faces unwashed since daybreak, with no desire to shower. Time had stopped. Mameh turned to stand by the door, and Nuraeni gradually stopped crying but didn't move. The smell of death had become less oppressive with the day's arrival, the sunlight slanting through the perforated ceiling, the lattices and the cracked walls.

It was one o'clock before they knew it, and Mameh went to the bathroom to piss. She opened the door without thinking, and dazzling daylight burst into the kitchen, while her feet moved on aimlessly, her nostrils widened to the fresh aroma of the front yard and its lush flowering shrubs. She stood on the terrace in her crumpled clothes and tangled hair, resembling a scarecrow hit by the previous night's storm, until their neighbor Jafar approached the house and stopped to consider Mameh's wretched appearance. They stared at each other. Mystified, Jafar thought the girl had lost her mind. Her eyes were blank and lusterless.

"What's wrong, kid?" Jafar asked.

The reply came out of nowhere, and Mameh didn't mean to phrase it this way: "My father is dead and rotting."

It took a while for Jafar to grasp what she meant.

"Oh God. Has it been weeks?"

"Last night."

Finally, here was someone to take care of the dank and putrid body before it really started to decompose. Jafar told Kyai Jahro, and then Ma Soma made an announcement over the surau's loudspeaker, bringing more of their neighbors to the house. Someone brought a divan and prepared buckets of water for the washing of the body. The gravedigger measured Komar's corpse with a bamboo pole and bummed a cigarette from the kyai. Before he left, Mameh told him to dig the grave right beside Marian's. Repeatedly, she insisted that he respect the dead man's wishes.

Even with the bustle of activity around them, the body being carried onto the terrace, to the well, and to the surau, Mameh and Nuraeni remained stupefied, staring numbly at what was happening or at nothing at all. Mameh was perhaps a little more lucid, talking to people, to some of her uncles, although she still hadn't combed her hair, changed her clothes, taken a shower or even washed her face. Nuraeni, on the other hand, was still in the kitchen. Now realizing that the moment for Komar bin Syueb to be buried was drawing nearer, she relapsed into grief and sobbing. No one bothered her, knowing her tendency to lose her wits. They would let her do as she liked, so long as she didn't insist on being buried, too.

This was when Margio returned home, his face shining as if the whole world were lit up by his presence. He took over the burial procession, the well-mannered child apparent once more, and went on to the surau to deliver the burial prayers. No one could fail to see how happy he was. Mameh picked flowers from their yard, all planted by Nuraeni, who was clearly unhappy with what she was doing. In some deft and complex manner, this crazy woman expressed both her grief and her objection to flowers being picked for her excuse of a husband. But Mameh didn't care. She kept plucking flowers, collecting them in a basket.

The coffin was covered by a golden sheet with silvery tassels, inscribed with the words of the Shahada. Kyai Jahro led the *salawat* chants as it left the surau, a few people following behind, mostly Margio's friends who had been hunting boars on the mountain and gave no thought to their mud-smeared clothes. Margio was among them, right next to the coffin, scattering the flowers Mameh had picked along the way. Komar bin Syueb was to be buried at the Budi Darma public cemetery, accompanied by frangipani and champak, a furious little Marian waiting for him on the other side.

They left, and the house was quiet again, save for the slowly fading *salawat* chants. Mameh and Nuraeni were returned to silence. Nuraeni had come out of the kitchen, looking hungry and stiff, but there was no food, so she dragged herself past the living room, slouched onto the terrace and sat on the divan where Komar had been washed. She could see that most of her favorite flowers had vanished. Mameh followed her with her eyes, still carrying the image of her miserable mother from that terrible night, when Nuraeni was near dead on that trunk, lying beneath her

70

husband, groaning like a cow with its throat cut. Suddenly a thought came. Mameh walked over to her, and spoke in a sharp voice.

"You should remarry, mother."

Nuraeni came to her senses and slapped her daughter hard. Mameh's cheek was hot and stinging.

Three

They moved to House 131 when Margio was seven, a trip he would later refer to as the Cow Family Joyride. It was a dramatic three-hour journey to a place Komar repeatedly called "our own house," passing along coral-paved paths that turned into swamps for the water buffaloes, which the family had to cross like the Jews at the parting of the Red Sea, a story Ma Soma would occasionally relate in the surau after teaching the Koran.

The family rode in a cart pulled by a pair of fat cows, borrowed at no cost from the owner of the rice mill. A truck was beyond their means. The man sat upfront, one hand dandling the reins ineffectively, the other energetically brandishing a whip to which the cows paid no heed. Beside him sat Nuraeni with little Mameh on her lap. Her head covered by a dark green veil with a silver floral motif, she tried to reassure her children as they whined about their relocation. Margio sat on the rolled-up mattresses, trying to keep their pan and buckets from falling off, despairing when a bump in the road threw their belongings to the ground. Margio would then have to get down to pick them up while the cart trundled on. Then he'd run after the cart, throw in the fallen objects, and leap back up, either to sit or lie down to watch the birds above.

There was actually a shortcut in the form of a wide asphalt road that hugged the coastline, much used by buses and trucks, but Komar bin Syueb worried about how the cows would react to the traffic. Instead, he pursued a meandering route, crossing hills, cutting through rice fields, passing through villages with rows of houses shaded by clumps of bamboo, the women out drying rice in the yards and the men collecting firewood. In every village people would stop working to stare in awe at the joyride, causing Nuraeni to sink deeper behind her veil, although Komar bin Syueb was unabashed. He said his hellos, and whenever someone asked where they were moving to, he would unhesitatingly reveal their destination.

Margio couldn't care less about the barefoot, half-naked children staring at them from the roadside. He was too busy reading his Mahabharata trading cards, chewing over which one was Arjuna and which Karna, and desperately trying to tell the twins Nakula and Sadewa apart. He was only disturbed when a poorly tethered teapot or bag of clothing sprang out as the wheels hit a fallen branch or a rock the size of someone's head. He did resent having to leave his previous home, losing the friends he traded cards and marbles with, who flew kites and went hunting for crickets with him. There was no guarantee that in the new place he would find anyone half as good.

Their home had stood at the intersection of two coral-paved roads, where a market was held every Monday. Once a week, it would be teeming with vendors setting out their baskets at the roadside or on terraces or filling up empty

74

lots. They sold coconuts, bananas, papayas and cassava, and some spread out beautiful clothes over wooden frames mounted on their bicycles. An old woman sold flowers in trays, and there were people leading cows, water buffaloes, and sheep they hoped to sell. There were chickens tied by their feet to ducks, and buckets of fish and eels. Women came here to shop, and small trucks were sometimes loaded up with produce, leaving almost nothing behind. If there was anyone outside on his terrace on days other than Monday, it was Komar bin Syueb the barber, set up with a large mirror leant against a table, a shaving kit, and a chair, with towels and cotton cutting capes hung from a few well-placed nails.

Home hadn't been a real house. It was nothing more than a coconut godown. Beside it stood a grand mansion, with large glass windows and a floor of glistening ivory tiles, scrubbed clean by the housemaid every day. Around it were orchards of rose-apple, orange, and mango trees, and a yard where two trucks were often parked overnight. One day the owner of the mansion had built a bigger godown behind his cooking-oil factory, and then mysteriously abandoned his wife and children. The original godown was left vacant until Komar and Nuraeni settled there—Margio still crouched in his mother's belly—renting it for the price of twelve heads on the shaving chair every month and with the obligation to look after the mansion together with the occupants.

Their home was a single concrete square a few feet on each side. The parents unrolled a mattress in this space—which had first to be purged of coconut fibers, scorpions, insects, and mice—and then crammed their bedding next to a bicycle, a closet, and a wicker mat to sit on. There was no kitchen. Nuraeni put the stove, the plate rack, and buckets beneath a melinjo tree behind their home. She had to surround her stove with a moldy little plywood fence to stop malevolent winds from blowing out the fire. After cooking, she would carry food containers, vegetable bowls, and a rice basket into the house, placing them next to the mattress, and they would eat there. There was no bathroom, obviously. Every morning and late afternoon they would go to the mansion, where they were lucky enough to be lent a bathroom and a toilet, separate from those used by the owner's wife and children. Margio and Mameh were born there, lived in such a fashion, and life seemed pretty good.

In their last few years at the godown, Margio's jobs were to fill the bathtub and to carry three buckets of water to the back terrace kitchen. He did this before going to school, and then again in the afternoon before heading to the beach to fly his kite. He made a lot of friends in the neighborhood, including the son of an ice vendor who was kind enough to supply him with popsicles. Then they moved to House 131.

The mansion's owner returned without warning, just as he had left. He sold the house, the orchards and, of course, the coconut godown, and moved his family away. Komar explored nearby areas, until he got lost near a soccer field, not far from the military base and the town market, and found that number 131 hadn't been occupied for eighteen months. He asked around to track down the owner and, when he found him, didn't have much trouble getting permission to live there, for the old owner thought the house was going to collapse. He returned to the godown with the news, but first had to persuade Nuraeni to hock her wedding ring to pay for the new house.

It wasn't easy to convince the kids to relocate, and even Nuraeni seemed unwilling, despite her years living without a kitchen or bathroom. Margio was the most stubborn. He pleaded to stay behind, and refused to understand that the mansion's new owner wouldn't lease them the godown, which he intended to turn into a shop selling toothbrushes, soap, and candy.

"Besides," Komar bin Syueb said, "we'll all be living in *our own* house."

Margio wasn't impressed. At seven years old, he was popular among his friends, leading them in eel hunts on joyful Sundays, selling the catch in the Monday market and taking the rest home to his mother. He went with the kids to collect firewood in the plantation, before it fell into neglect, and it was Margio among the boys who had to muster the courage to confront the foreman when he raised a stink because the boys knocked down the unripe fruits as they tore at the dead coconut fronds. He would sell the firewood, since his mother didn't use a wood stove, and with the money he could buy marbles, as well as paper and thread to make kites. Plus he had more boxes of crickets than any kid his age. Little Margio thought he had it made, and viewed the move with grave suspicion.

He sulked and threatened to run away. He would stay put even if it meant sleeping on a neighbor's terrace, or in a shed in the cacao plantation. Finally, Komar dragged him to a corner of the godown and gave him a talking-to, calling him an ungrateful brat. Margio said nothing, so Komar bin Syueb told him to speak, and when Margio was about to open his mouth his father saw something insolent in his expression and landed a biting slap on his face. His cheeks reddened and his eyes turned wet, but Margio never let himself cry. He said nothing. Infuriated by his silence, Komar grabbed the rattan cane used to beat the mattress and slapped it against his son's calf, making Margio slump against the wall with one leg up. He could resist, but he was going to lose.

And so the mattress was rolled up, bound tightly with a plastic rope, and stacked on the cart over a sheet of wicker matting. The plate rack was attached at the rear, while the plates and glasses were in a basket, wrapped with fabric and pillows. The shaving kit was folded and hidden under a bag filled with their clothes, which was crammed in with the chairs and tables, their pan and buckets, a stove, and bowls. Margio sandwiched his boxes of crickets and marbles between the pillows, while the rubber-band-tied trading cards were stuffed into the pocket of the crimson-red school uniform shorts he was wearing. He stood there by the cow cart, in a shirt missing two buttons, his hair stiff and reddish, his slippers mismatched, until Komar told him to hop on once the tailgate was shut and they had said their goodbyes.

If he were to recall the saddest day of his life, this would be it. Margio could see his mother's reluctant face behind a veil she had never worn before, sat next to Komar. Margio wondered whether she was more upset about moving or losing her wedding ring. He had thought of his mother as an ally, but her silence made him realize how little help she would be, and in frustration he climbed onto the cart and perched on the mattress, watched by his friends, who were standing on the terrace where Komar bin Syueb had been plying his trade all these years.

They weren't really going far, but the cows' sluggish pace and the choice of route dragged out the journey. Later on, Margio could walk to his old haunts and visit friends. Now mostly silent on the mattress, he sometimes lay on his back to stare at clouds or passing herons, sometimes turned to look at the meandering road behind him, stretching far into the distance, or propped his chin on his hands to watch the rolling pungent rice fields. Nuraeni didn't say anything either, holding herself hunched as if tortured with shame. When they passed someone on the road, she gave no sign of acknowledgment. She might have been a newlywed guarding her dignity, except in her arms she held a daughter who, despite the rattling of the cart, slept like a log. Later on Margio would tell his sister how lucky she had been to sleep through this humiliating journey.

Komar bin Syueb alone sat upright, every once in a while entertaining himself with a song. Now and then they took a break when the two cows seemed tired. Meantime, the passengers would have a drink and eat bananas and fried rice crust.

When they emerged onto an asphalt street, Komar announced that they were almost there. Behind them in the mud were the parallel tracks of the cart's rubber-rimmed wooden wheels. They had reached the outskirts of town, an avenue of beautiful houses. They had yet to see their new home, but at this welcome sight, at the glistening colored fences embellished with ornate ironwork, bright lights, and mailboxes, Margio started to get excited. He glanced at his mother, hoping to see his feelings mirrored there. But Nuraeni remained hunkered deep inside herself. Margio forgot her when he looked again at the people on their terraces, the hanging pots of elephant-ear plants, and orchids growing on posts. Which house would they stop at?

79

But instead of stopping here they turned into an alley so narrow the cart almost couldn't get through. Margio had to pull back the plate rack, which stuck out and bumped against the fences. The cart trundled more slowly than ever, more shakily, past densely packed shacks and untended gardens, all previously hidden by the bright houses they had passed. Finally, they stopped under a kapok tree that had just shed its flowers. Number 131 stood before them.

"Here's the house," said Komar, with a pride that met no response from his family.

The house was bigger than their old godown, measuring perhaps forty feet a side, so there had to be a bedroom, a kitchen, and a bathroom. But Margio reckoned one wicked storm would be more than enough to blow it away. A falling coconut could flatten it. At a glance you could see it was tilting to one side, on the verge of collapse. It looked somber and smelled of death, damp, and misery. The roof was made of faded red clay tiles, blackened by the sun-baked moss. Margio bet the water came slithering down right into the heart of the house when it rained. The walls, made of bamboo wickerwork, were warped and moved in the wind. The old lime coating had flaked off, baring the cut sections of each piece of bamboo.

Komar opened the padlock hanging on the front door while his family stood behind him, dumbfounded with disappointment. Swelled by the summer humidity, the door didn't open easily. One they had opened it, the damn thing wouldn't close properly. Inside it was dark and reeked of rotten garbage, neglected for eighteen months, hosting spider webs and feeding the rats, who scurried away at the sound of their footsteps. A startled bat flapped around the room before escaping. The pervading smell of bat and gecko shit faded a little with the breeze once the windows were open.

The floor was nothing but dank dirt, gritty against the soles of their feet. Margio had been right about the rainwater dripping into the house. They couldn't possibly unroll the wicker mat and the mattress on the floor as in the previous house. They would have to get two bedframes.

"Is there anything more battered than this?" Nuraeni said, opening her mouth for the first time.

"Oh, shut up. Battered as it may be, it's our own home," Komar replied.

Nuraeni should have known how little they would get for a six-carat wedding ring. The house was theirs, although the land it stood on was not.

For a whole week they cleaned up, brushing away spider webs and catching rats that teemed inside nests that they swiftly plugged up. Komar borrowed a hoe to level the floor and to clear it of various animal droppings. He climbed onto the roof with Margio to fix the tiles disturbed by the wind and the pigeons. Margio's resentment deepened. Yet there wasn't much he could do other than follow his father's instructions, else he would have to face the rattan cane a second time. They also had to cut away the ferns and fungi, and chop down the coral tree by the well at the back.

They were lucky to get a well, although they had to clean that too before a rope-and-bucket system was installed. The bathroom was the most luxurious thing in the house, made of a cement base mixed with fragments of ceramic tiles, with a clogged toilet that took a month to fix. Until then they had to shit in the cacao plantation or a small ditch behind the brick factory. The house had two bedrooms, for which Komar brought two wooden beds one morning, one for himself, Nuraeni, and little Mameh, and the other for Margio. Later on this changed. One room belonged to Nuraeni and Mameh, and the other to Komar bin Syueb. Margio was relegated to the divan in the living room, the nightwatch hut, the surau, or Agus Sofyan's stall.

The land itself belonged to an old woman named Ma Rabiah who, like Anwar Sadat's wife Kasia, owned land that stretched past the borders of several villages. The houses along the side of the big road had been built on lots successfully acquired from the previous owner. That had happened back when families would come and go, bringing frameworks for their houses, which looked as if they could all be folded and packed into sacks. Some of the newcomers on the narrow road never told Ma Rabiah what they were doing until she saw for herself the white houses stood there, the front yards adorned by beautiful jasmine trees. Should any squatters decide to move on, they would dislodge the bamboo walls, roll them up, and carry them away along with the house's wooden framework, and then someone would come to take their place.

"Here we are, waiting until Ma Rabiah kicks us out, when we'll have to roll all this stuff up again," said Nuraeni, once they had made the house livable.

In her whole life, Ma Rabiah had never evicted a soul. The settlers came and went as they pleased. The old granny never even collected rent or came to ask for help with the taxes. She liked to talk about other matters and to pass the hours chortling away with other women before going home. She was the kind, old widow of an army veteran, and the only compensation the squatters gave their landlady was the tins of

82

biscuits sent to her home every Eid ul-Fitr. She never asked for them, nor were her decaying teeth up to eating them.

Many years before, when the area was nothing but a jungle of shrubs except for where the fishermen lived along the shore, those plots of land had no owners at all. The first settlers were a band of nomads from the east who divided the land among themselves with boundary stakes. These people, said to be twelve men who arrived on donkeys, valiantly chased away the boars and the ajaks, set up houses and farms for the first time, and became owners of land that spread out past boundaries unseen. They awed the fishermen who congregated along the banks of the rivers. They cut down the bushes, cultivated rice, and came to be remembered as the founders of the township.

They brought in beautiful women, from the fishing villages and elsewhere, married them and their children inherited the land: the farms, rice fields, and coconut plantations. One of these founder families produced Ma Rabiah, and another spawned Kasia. Kasia came from the fourth generation of the boundary stakes people, while Ma Rabiah was said to come from the third, even though what she owned almost couldn't be calculated or charted, even after she divided the land among her cousins. When Komar bin Syueb came to reside there, the stakes were said still to stand where they were first planted.

As a girl Ma Rabiah married a soldier during the fledgling years of the Republic, and they lived quite prosperously without having to rely on her land, supporting themselves through open smuggling activities controlled by the local military. This lasted right through the revolution years and beyond. Mayor Sadrah could confirm all this as true. Thus the myriad pieces of land went to seed in the hands of two people who probably forgot even owning them. The lands reverted to a jungle of shrubs where cogongrass and reeds flourished wildly—until the day people began to arrive as the town took shape, regarding with wonder the endless parcels of neglected land. They came to Ma Rabiah's house, hoping to rent or buy, but since she didn't need money, she told them to live there for free. But some owners of the houses along the big road insisted on paying, because they didn't want to be disturbed or evicted, and because they could afford it.

Ma Rabiah and her husband had eight children, all of them well known among the townsfolk for their ruthless entrepreneurship. One of them was the first to build a cinema with screenings three times a day, every day of the week. Another opened a donut shop, advertising the number-one donuts in the world. Still another set up a shrimp factory, or rather bought up shrimp and fish from all the fishermen along half the southern coast, to be resold to shrimp-eating nations. People referred to his giant tanks and freezers as a factory. All these children traveled around in shiny cars and became the town's celebrities, as well as nightmares to those squatting on their mother's property.

Not long after their father's death, the siblings began to wrangle over land inheritance, not caring in the least that these plots belonged to their living mother. The eldest kicked out a family that had resided there for eighteen years. Indifferent to their pleas, he was going to build an ice factory. The family had to disassemble their home and move. Envious of the actions of the eldest, the younger siblings evicted several other families, making way for shops, factories, and fishponds, or simply letting some plots deteriorate into lairs for evil spirits. They set up new boundary stakes, dividing the land among themselves without consulting their mother.

No one uttered a word of complaint to Ma Rabiah, but she could read what she saw in her tenants' eyes. She had always enjoyed surveying her empire, walking from shack to shack and communing with her people. But now she was alarmed by the actions of eight ungrateful brats. She rebuked them for their arrogance in evicting people without telling her, but they were more obstinate than the devil himself, worse than she had ever imagined. Not only did they refuse to apologize, they retaliated with even more evictions.

Hurt by her children, she would say to various people: "Find me a way to write them out of my will."

One day the plan arrived in a moment of inspiration. She'd been going from one house to the next, sitting with the men and women, telling them she was going to sell her land, that they would have to pay for the plots they occupied. Every one of her tenants, including Komar, wished they could call the land their own, but not many had the money. At some point in her travels through the neighborhood, Ma Rabiah arrived at one obvious, simple solution.

"I'll sell it as *cheaply* as possible."

For Komar, *cheaply* meant he had to shave as many as one hundred and twenty heads pay for the land where his house stood and for the small front garden. It was their eighth year here, and Komar had been saving money to recover the wedding ring he had pawned, although until the day he died he never managed to retrieve it. The other neighbors withdrew their modest savings, borrowed money from Makojah, the town's moneylender, or sold their motorbikes and necklaces, so that in a year the plots of land quickly changed hands.

Transfer deeds were written up, signed, marked with the old woman's thumbprint, and sealed with revenue stamps. People's worries faded away. The day when they would have to fold their houses into sacks would never come. Their deeds were framed and hung in their living rooms, like degree certificates, their most valuable possessions. Their love for Ma Rabiah grew, even if a tin of unwanted biscuits was its only expression.

The sums paid were small, but cumulatively the deeds marked with Ma Rabiah's thumbprint added up to real wealth. She had never thought she would be truly rich, but the money was now literally piled under her bed. Even if she wanted to hide it somewhere safe, she would have no idea where. She worried her eight children would learn about the money scattered around her home, and then she found a solution. What she did would cause a sensation among the townsfolk for years to come, and would evolve into a tale passed between generations along with the town's other legends.

In the few remaining days of her old age, Ma Rabiah splashed out on a pair of horses, so gentle the children played with them, which she let loose by the seashore. She also bought a bus because, as people said, ever since her child-hood she'd always loved riding on buses. But because she couldn't drive it, the vehicle just sat behind her house and became a chicken coop. One day she went to the cinema belonging to one of her sons without telling him, and bought up all the tickets to watch the film alone. Everyone still remembers that film, *Puteri Giok*, because she then bought up more tickets so that people could go see it free of charge for the next two days. Not quite done with her splurge, she went to a clothes shop and bought five wedding gowns she would never wear, except for one she slept in that very night and another for when she died. She bought a sack of bread and shared the contents with some little kids, and finished the remnants while riding a tricycle, on which she pedaled home in gales of laughter.

Her children only found out what was going on after a series of unsuccessful attempts to dismantle several houses. The newly titled owners stopped the evictions in their tracks by holding up the framed transfer deeds. It was only then they saw the horses cantering in the wild and with horror noticed the bus full of chicken shit. To top it all, the cinema manager ratted on their mother. Infuriated, the children plotted together to grab whatever was left, drew up a long letter saying she would bequeath them what remained, and tried to force Ma Rabiah to impress her thumbprint upon it. Dismayed, the old woman shook her head, refusing to give in.

As would be remembered forever, that morning Ma Rabiah wore one of her wedding gowns for the last time, having rejected her children's rough entreaties. She sat on a small bench before her house, eating the soil in her frontyard lump by lump. Some people tried to stop her, but she insisted she was better off eating the land, rather than letting it fall into the hands of her damned children, who cared more for their mother's wealth than for her. All the while she kept on scooping soil into her mouth. Someone reported all this to the children, as well as to the police and the officers at the military base. But by the time they arrived she was sprawled

87

out in her beautiful satin and lace wedding dress, cold and lifeless. Somebody said she had choked on a handful of gravel. Ma Rabiah's stubbornness in guarding the land to her death became legendary.

That's how Komar bin Syueb came to own his house and the land it stood on. He never ceased to be surprised by this good fortune. Though still unquestionably poor, he had reached a level of affluence he always thought beyond him. Now he no longer gave haircuts on the terrace, but at the market instead, waiting with his bike under a tropical almond tree, next to a chicken and noodle stall, before handing the spot to a *bajigur* vendor who sold hot, sweet coconut milk at night.

Despite this good luck, Margio and Nuraeni never forgot their initial disappointment at finding House 131 no better than a lair for evil spirits, and as a young girl the family's deed of ownership brought Mameh no happiness. In reality not much had changed in the eight years they had been living there, except that Margio and Mameh had grown, and Nuraeni become more shrunken and disheveled.

Those who had known her since her childhood could see how far she had deteriorated. You only had to glance at her long-expired identity card, printed early in her marriage, and the beautiful woman pictured there, all curly hair and plump cheeks, radiant round eyes glowing. Compare that to her appearance now, a faded beauty, her eyes grey and dim, her cheeks hollow, and her fair skin no longer radiant but chalky. Nothing expressed her discontent more eloquently than her wasted looks. Komar bin Syueb knew it very well. The day he told Nuraeni the land was theirs she was no more thrilled than she would have been had he returned home with three kilos of rice.

"At least now you can plant it with flowers and no one will ever cut them down," said Komar, trying to arouse her enthusiasm.

The enthusiasm never came. Nuraeni simply hid away in the kitchen, as she often did these days to avoid her husband. She sat on a small stool in front of the stove. Komar had registered her new habit and understood what it meant. He watched her talking to the stove and pan. At first he thought she was just moaning inarticulately, muttering noises not intended to be understood, but as the days passed it became clear that Nuraeni was actually conversing with these inanimate objects, engaged in conversations no one else could understand.

This was when he decided his wife had lost her wits. But perhaps she was just pretending to be crazy, since she behaved normally most of the time and could be coaxed into conversation. She still complained about this and that, told the kids to do their chores, berated Mameh for forgetting to sweep the house, or called Margio to shoo a gecko away. But quite often she would become unbalanced and recognize no one but herself. Komar saw this as lunacy, and her craziness seemed to be getting worse, as both Mameh and Margio would later discover.

He had married Nuraeni when she was sixteen years old and he was nearly thirty. As was common in the village, the match was an arranged one, and the engagement had lasted four years. On the day Syueb came with a pail full of rice and noodles and a dark blue scarf to ask for her hand in marriage on behalf of Komar, she was a girl whose breasts were only budding and with hair still sparse between her legs. Of course, the two fathers had discussed the matter already, meaning that even this proposal was arranged, a formality. They agreed that once Nuraeni was able to bear a child, the two would be married in the nearest surau. Present at the time were Syueb and the girl's father, their wives, and a couple of other relatives, whereas Komar was off somewhere, perhaps in the big city looking for work, like most of the local young men, and Nuraeni was probably out washing clothes at the water spout or searching for clams with her friends.

The girl wasn't told until dusk. Her father said, "*Nyai*, one day you will marry Komar bin Syueb."

She really didn't know the man at all, aware of him only as someone in the village, a name to which she could barely attach a face. The fact it was him didn't surprise her, because she had no expectations. Like every other girl, she had been waiting for the moment her father would tell her who she would marry, but there was no young man she favored over the others. The news itself was enough to make the twelve-year-old girl happy, despite the inevitable fear of what would follow. At least now Nuraeni was able to tell her closest friends she had a fiancé. Nothing was more embarrassing for a girl older than twelve than not knowing who would be her husband.

The evening changed many things, because little Nuraeni had become the young woman Nuraeni. Her mother bought her crimson lipstick and an eyebrow pencil, and she no longer let her slightly protruding breasts be exposed in the breezy air of the hillside village. The news rippled out swiftly, reaching the ears of relatives and friends, of the girl whose fate was half bound with Komar bin Syueb's, and they felt happy for her.

She no longer followed her father to the rice fields in the morning, to stand on the plough so it sank into the mud while two buffaloes walked slowly along the plots, splattering her with earth. Nor would she lead their two sheep to the grassland on the hillside, herding them with the other shepherd kids, carrying two dry coconut stems as firewood on the way home. No, these tasks were now her younger brothers', while she stayed at her mother's side. In the morning she would light the grill to cook rice and learn every aspect of making the perfect *lodeh* dish. She still went to the rice fields, not to till the land, but to scatter seeds that had been soaked overnight. When their light green spikes shot up, she would join the other women to pull them out and plant them in the plots drawn with crisscrossing lines by her father and younger brothers. As they waited for the rice to grow tall, her father and brothers spread the fertilizer and kept watch on the water lest it turn stagnant, and she and her mother would carry the lunch hamper to a hut by a levee. She would return to the fields with her mother again when the algae and weeds needed clearing, and there would also be a time for her to harvest the ripe grains with an *ani-ani* knife, back in the days before the villagers used sickles. Other than that, Nuraeni had to look after her body in order for it to blossom, and to mind her language. For now she had a fiancé and was preparing for her wedding.

As for Komar, in keeping with local conventions, he had left his village shortly after turning twenty, since there wasn't much to do at home for men of his age. Syueb had several plots of both wet and dry fields, but he could manage them with his wife without help, and had all the time he needed to serve as the only barber in the village. After a short lesson on how to shave people's heads, how to use a blade to trim mustaches and stubble, and after several attempts to replace his father, Komar followed a friend and wandered out into the world, equipped with the knowledge of how to shave a man's chin. Naturally, at first he didn't want to be a barber at all, and hoped to get a job at some factory instead, like other young men.

He would come home once a year, before Eid ul-Fitr, more commonly called Lebaran, together with many other young men and wandering families, who during this great homecoming would appear in rows on the hilly path, with cardboard boxes and bags in their hands or on their shoulders. His hair was greasy with pomade, and he sported a shirt with the sleeves rolled up to the elbows, corduroy pants still smelling of the barbershop, a watch, and a pair of black leather shoes that prompted him to tread carefully around the ubiquitous mud holes.

In his large bag was tobacco for Syueb, a batik skirt for his mother, pretty gowns for his younger sisters and, since he'd heard about his engagement, a present for his future wife as well. She was a stranger to him, but he knew she was beautiful and welcomed the marriage. He remembered the day the girl was born, because he'd been playing right next to her house and had watched people gather in anticipation of the baby's delivery. He'd seen Nuraeni several times when she was a schoolgirl, since the school wasn't far from his house. But his knowledge of her didn't stretch much beyond her long, curly, dark hair, often tied back with a ribbon, a pointed nose, plump cheeks, and gleaming round eyes. When someone told him that his father had chosen the girl for him, sure enough Komar dreamed about her every night, until he decided to come home earlier than usual.

They met on the eve of Lebaran. Komar gave her a tin of biscuits and a pretty pink purse, and bashfully handed her a photo of himself. He was pictured posing in front of a bright yellow Volkswagen Kombi, which obviously wasn't his and was clearly sitting in a parking lot. He looked awkward with one hand half sunk in a pocket, but his expression was cheerful and rather proud, as if no one could contrive a better pose and location.

They spent the whole Lebaran day together, going from houses to house, shaking hands with neighbors and relatives, and bragging that they were soon to be husband and wife, just as other couples were doing who had only met that day. Komar and Nuraeni walked side by side, stopping many times to greet passersby, the couple blushing from a mixture of joy and embarrassment. Nuraeni held on tightly to her pink purse, while Komar couldn't really decide where to put his hands, first slipping them into the pockets of his corduroy pants, then folding them across his chest, and finally letting them hang clasped behind his back, as it certainly wasn't yet time for them to hold hands. Even the slightest touch would make both of them shiver, their faces reddening.

Komar took her to try Wa Dullah's meatballs at the noodle stall, which had a reputation for quality and high prices. It stood by the river in a row of stalls where people waited for the ferry. Customers jostled to be served, and when the couple's order came they found a big rock to sit on, and ate there, holding the bowl with one hand and the spoon with the other. At one point Komar slipped, and a meatball was flipped into the air, and they giggled, warm and full of love, the way it should be at the beginning. In the afternoon they had grilled fish at a shack under a hog plum tree, after fishing with some friends at Wa Haji's ponds. It was the habit of the locals to bring cooked rice wrapped in banana leaves to his land on the hillside, and fish there and cook the catch without going home. Days passed, but it felt like their time together would never end.

One night Komar took Nuraeni with a group of friends to see a play at the village theater. After Lebaran the theater would always be packed, since there was little to do at night unless you traveled far away to another town. They would always remember the play's title, *Titian Rambut Dibelah Tujuh*, though the other details became blurred. It was about a heartless son, rather like the humble folk hero Malin Kundang, who becomes so rich and proud that he rejects his own mother and is turned to stone. At the office was a poster of a man burning in Hell. They would never forget that evening, because it was the first time they touched. In the dark, sat on a plank bench, they held hands. Not squeezing, just holding and that was enough to make them sizzle as if a fire had been lit in their bellies. That night they went home and both dreamt of being bitten by a snake.

Not too long after Lebaran, Komar had to resume his wanderings with his friends and earn some money, and Nuraeni accompanied him to the village hall with tears in her eyes. She thought she was truly in love, and hoped the wedding would be soon. But Komar convinced her he had to go, and that he would definitely be back for next year's Lebaran. Bags were piled up on the hall floor, full of clothes, pineapples, green bananas, and snacks the mothers made for their sons to eat on their journey. Before Komar left to cross the hills for the ferry, Nuraeni made a short plea in simple words spoken by every one of the abandoned girls: "Write to me."

The letters usually arrived on Mondays at ten in the morning. A postman would come on foot, his bag on his shoulder, his shoes always smeared with maroon clay, to hand out letters at the village hall. Treated to warm sweet tea and potato chips, he would remain there half an hour before returning the way he had come. The girls would wait in front of the hall; some would receive letters from their fiancés, while others sulked in disappointment, remaining hopeful that next week would be different. Of course there would always be letters for other people in the village, but believe me, the numbers were insignificant.

The Monday after Komar left, Nuraeni was busying herself from dawn in anticipation of his letter. She cleaned the house and mopped the floor so she could get to the village hall early. In those days most of the houses stood on stilts, with wicker flooring that needed mopping every day to keep away the grime and dust. When her father returned from the surau, the floor was already glistening in the glow of the wick lamp. Nuraeni rushed to the kitchen, lighting the stove with coconut fibers, blowing on it through a bamboo shaft to get it blazing, and stoking the fire with pieces of firewood as the flames danced. She heated some water on the stove, and while waiting for it to boil, she washed some rice and let her mother do the rest, because she had to hurry to the water spout to wash their clothes and dirty dishes.

The girl was nimble and swift in everything she did that day, carrying a bucket of dirty laundry in one hand and a pail full of dirty plates and glasses in the other. Her family owned a fishpond by the water spout where they showered and did the washing, with water flushing through bamboo pipes stretching for miles all the way up to the springs in the hills. The spout was surrounded by a chest-high wall, with sugar palm leaves for a roof, and served as the family's bathroom. As she did the washing, her father fed the fish with taro leaves plucked from the pond's levee.

The sun rose as Nuraeni finished the dishes and tossed the kitchen leftovers into the pond, the fish competing for the remnants of rice and stale food making the water bubble. Sunlight dappled the ground. Some villagers in tattered shirts and worn-out shorts walked by carrying hoes with which to wrestle the earth, while others checked their dry fields and gathered wood with machetes. A floating mist crept up toward the hilltops, as the shrill voices of girls chatting across the distance between two waterspouts drowned out the sparrows and woodpeckers. Schoolchildren lined the fishpond levee, throwing pebbles into the water, bags swinging behind their backs and caps covering their little heads.

Nuraeni took off her clothes, threw them on top of the wicker wall, and modestly covered the entrance to the spout with a towel, although the plaited bamboo strips didn't conceal her shape entirely. Holding her knees, she sat under the plentiful and sparkling water pouring from the bamboo pipe, wet hair draping her body. Washing away the sweat, the shower lifted her spirits, as she rubbed her skin with soap, checking the creases between each toe, scrubbing off the dirt, rinsing her hair with aloe, and remaining sat under the spout, just as she was, as she brushed her teeth.

The chatter of the girls at the other spouts faded; they were leaving, and perhaps some of them were already packing the village hall's veranda, waiting for the exhausted postman.

Nuraeni stepped out of the cabin, dried herself, and wrapped a towel around her body, covering the top of her thighs and her unripe breasts. She coiled her hair up, picked up the bucket of wet laundry with one hand and the pail of sparkling plates and glasses with the other, and moved with catlike steps, treading on the levees between the ponds, exquisite under the rising sun. She was unconscious of her beauty.

Just before ten o'clock Nuraeni was at the hall, with her damp hair in two neat braids and tied with a faded yellow bow at each end. She had guessed right. The other girls were already cramming the long bench under the announcement board bearing last Ramadan's timetable as well as other information that could easily be ignored. Some girls who didn't get a seat gathered under a mussaenda tree by the bamboo fence, and Nuraeni joined them to exchange funny stories about Lebaran.

And yet she was still thinking about the letter, because this was the first time she had ever waited for a letter from a man. Her heart was pounding. What kind of surprise would that first letter hold? Ugly handwriting, perhaps. Even this was enough to feed her excitement. Maybe it would be sprinkled with scented powder, like the letters her best friend, Nyai Sri, got from her boyfriend.

What happened was entirely unexpected. The exhausted postman arrived with a stack of letters held together with an elastic band. The girls spread them on a table while the postman fanned himself with an old newspaper. Girls yelped upon finding their names on those white envelopes with blue-and-red stripes along the edges, while others snorted in disappointment having found nothing addressed to them. Nuraeni was among the persistent searchers who scoured the few unclaimed letters remaining, most of them addressed to the village head and a few to parents from their children. She stood looking at the scattered envelopes, almost in tears. None of the letters was for her. She went home with red eyes and lips pursed shut, thinking desperately of the following Monday. She had never known bitterness like this, and it was all because of Komar.

She grew increasingly distressed with the absence of a letter the following week, and the next, and in the weeks thereafter. The other girls might miss out on a letter now and then, but at least once a month one would turn up. Some would get beautiful presents; one or two were sent the money to buy a ring, while others might find sewing machines with their names on. One girl was even sent a wedding dress, but there was never anything for Nuraeni.

After a few agonizing weeks, she stopped going to the village hall. The photo of Komar posing before the Kombi, which she had framed and placed next to her bed, now lay inside a tattered box under her bed. At first she had wanted to rip it up and throw it into a blazing stove. She stopped hoping for anything, didn't want to talk about him, let alone allow him to toy with her imagination by intruding on her daydreams, and if he sneaked into her sleep, the dream would turn into an aggravating nightmare.

As time passed, she began to suspect that Komar didn't really love her and had no intention of marrying her. Just think, she said to herself, last Lebaran he didn't take her to that photo studio near the Koranic school. He clearly didn't want her picture in his wallet, and felt it was sufficient to leave her a blurred picture of himself, probably taken from a distance with an instant camera. She was jealous of the other girls, who had gone with their boyfriends to the Tan Brothers studio, the only Chinese family they knew, wearing lovely dresses, powder, and lipstick, and standing before a flood-light—or so the girls told her—to get their photos taken against a backdrop of swans upon a pond.

With time all hope that the wedding would happen vanished. She was a little girl again, although she didn't resume ploughing the rice fields or herding sheep. She no longer bothered with primping herself and looked forward to the time when, through some good fortune, the engagement would be broken. Then maybe another man would propose, a man who would send her letters, take her to be photographed, and maybe even give her a beautiful ring and a sewing machine so she could learn to make her own wedding dress.

She went about life as if she didn't have a fiancé, and painfully she had to mask her situation. Perhaps a few friends knew the truth, but she tried to convince herself they were too busy with their own lives to realize that someone among them had been spurned by her fiancé. When people asked for news of Komar—and Syueb himself would visit to find out this or that about the bad manners of his son—Nuraeni would tell them he was fine, but he wasn't coming home before the next Lebaran. She felt like a know-it-all witch who could spy on her lover through a small mirror, and if that were indeed the case, she would love to throw rocks at him and hit him with a rice-pounder, because nothing else would show how much she resented that man.

Lebaran came round again, but Nuraeni awaited it not with a blossoming heart, but with an icy will. She had promised herself not to ask for an explanation. She didn't even think about welcoming him, and if he did come around she'd treat him like a distant guest who had dropped by to ask for a drink. There would be no nostalgia and no soft sentiments. Komar would have to pay a high price for the way he mistreated her.

Komar finally did swing by. His greasy, pomaded hair was unchanged, and he wore the same old wristwatch, although the corduroy pants had been replaced with blue jeans held up by a faux leather belt, and he wasn't wearing a shirt, but a long-sleeved T-shirt. This year he had grown a mustache and a beard, and had let them become unkempt. He offered no explanation for his silence, just as there was no beautiful purse for Nuraeni, only a tin of biscuits. Last year he had been very polite, sitting and blushing nervously; now he was loutish, and sat facing her with one foot on top of the other. His hands eagerly reached for a clove cigarette, lighting it and letting it crackle, prompting Nuraeni quickly to put an ashtray in front of him.

Asking no questions, Nuraeni put a glass of cold lemonade next to the ashtray and just sat in her chair playing with her fingernails. No news was exchanged and there was no sweet talk. Komar even opened the tin of biscuits he had brought and shamelessly took one for himself while babbling about Wa Haji's fish last year.

That night, despite her resentment, Nuraeni went to the theater with him, to spare the feelings of his father and his future parents-in-law, in case they sensed that she was acting coldly toward her husband-to-be. This time they went to see *Nyai Dasima*. The title stuck in their minds, but not the actors' names, because acting companies came and went in the village. For Nuraeni it was her third visit. She had seen a different play with a group of girlfriends on the

100

carnival-filled night of Independence Day. Nothing special happened during the show, except for Komar trying to squeeze her hand. But something sickening happened on the way home.

They slowed down to let their friends go ahead, and in a quiet spot Komar shamelessly asked Nuraeni for a kiss. Shocked by the unexpected request, Nuraeni cringed and shook her head in fear, but Komar gripped her hand and insisted. "No," she said. Komar persisted. "Just a little kiss," he implored, "one tiny touch." There seemed to be no other choice. To scream would only humiliate them both, and she supposed Komar wouldn't go any further, since far behind them were other people walking in the same direction. Without saying yes or no, she let his mouth attack her own, as he pushed her against a hibiscus tree. His lips pressed against hers in a long-drawn-out kiss. His wet open mouth smelt of tobacco and nipped at her lips with tiny, tugging bites. Afterwards, Nuraeni felt nauseous.

Their former intimacy was lost, and Nuraeni remained icy the next day. For the sake of good manners, she saw him off at the village hall the next day, and there, inconsolable at the memory of the letters that never came, Nuraeni asked him for nothing. Instead, it was Komar who spoke up:

"Aren't you curious about my job?"

Why should she care about his job if he didn't care to think about her, the way she ached for news from him week after week until she felt all worn and rusted inside. She stared at him, her eyes sharp and almost cruel, twisting the lips he had once crushed with a kiss. Flaunting her disdain, she finally opened her mouth: "So what is it?"

"A barber," Komar replied.

Going so far away just to be a barber, Nuraeni thought. She couldn't care less whether Komar were a bandit, a bully, a thug, or a thief. A year of disappointment had exhausted her love, and what he did was of no interest. When Komar, bag in hand, walked away to join the other migrant workers, Nuraeni didn't do more than nod slightly to acknowledge his departure, this time without glistening red eyes or a stream of tears. As soon as Komar disappeared at the foot of the hills, she rushed to the spout to shower. Only now he was gone did she bother to pay attention to her appearance.

All that happened, and yet at the age of sixteen she allowed herself to be hustled off and married to that man. Komar's gift was a six-gram gold ring engraved with their initials, and he always bragged it was the work of a well-known and skilled local engraver. Nuraeni wore a traditional white blouse, her hair tied into a high bun, and displayed a disdain she would have been disappointed to learn was flattering. Komar wore a black suit and a borrowed black hat (a peci), and Wa Haji officiated as *penghulu*. Nuraeni's father gave up one of his ewes for slaughter, since it had already given birth to five lambs, which were now getting big. He also dug up all the rice in the family storage chest. There was no *wayang*— or shadow puppet—performance, but there was enough food that the guests could take some home.

From the first night, the marriage was one of hatred. Nuraeni lay exhausted in bed, still in her wedding blouse, her hips and legs tightly bound in a batik skirt. The lust-ridden Komar invited her to get naked so they could make love, but Nuraeni merely growled, half-awake, remaining wrapped-up and defensive. Without another word Komar stripped off his clothes, keeping on the underpants that swelled with his erection, and shoved his newlywed to wake her. Nuraeni rolled over, groaned, and reached for the bolster. Annoyed, Komar began to yank at her skirt, tugging at it until his wife was clumsily unrolled. The skirt undone, he discovered a pair of light-green panties with a floral design. Komar pinned her down, lowering first her underwear and next his own, and then thrust into her. They fucked without words until they ached and finally fell asleep. Having lost her virginity, Nuraeni retrieved her skirt, covered herself up, and turned her back on her husband, keeping her legs apart because of the smarting between them.

A week later, Komar went to look for a place for them to live together, and a month after that took Nuraeni to the coconut godown near the Monday Market. He provided a mattress, a stove, kitchen utensils, a table and chairs, and his shaving kit. They owned a Dutch bike, which Komar bought from the flea market in front of their terrace. Nuraeni's quality of life had deteriorated, but she dealt with it without complaint.

Sex was always difficult. Nuraeni shared none of Komar's eagerness, and when his lust built until he felt it constrict his throat, he would frequently force himself on her. When that happened, he was brutal. He threw her on the mattress, and fucked her with her clothes on. On other occasions, he would make her lie with her legs apart on the table or have her crouch in the bathroom. When Nuraeni tried to resist, he would beat her. A slap to the face was a common occurrence, and at times he kicked her beautiful calves, sending her tumbling helplessly to the floor. Only then could Komar get between her legs.

To Nuraeni, her husband's treatment felt like slow death,

but she didn't know what to do. She never thought of leaving him and going back to her father. Her family would have been furious. All she could do was keep to herself, and since sometimes Komar could be sweet and treat her well, hope didn't die entirely. No matter how hard things became, she never gave in to self-pity, a stoic resolve she would pass on to her children.

Margio was a child of domestic rape, yet the boy seemed to be an infinite consolation to Nuraeni, and her husband's brutality lessened with his arrival. His birth put a dampener on Komar's lust, and his mother loved him even more for that. He was a source of joy to them both. But with the passing of time, as the little boy began to grow, crawl, and walk, Komar's desire returned. It surged and made him shiver. He would wait to catch Nuraeni off guard and jump on her. He was a savage again. She tried her best never to let him see her naked, but it did nothing to deter him. He would take any opportunity to pull up her skirt, slip her panties down, and then, standing by the door, to penetrate her with a wiggling of his buttocks. It was the old regime returned, complete with ruthless slaps and swings of the water dipper. Nuraeni became pregnant again, and Mameh was born two years after Margio.

Eight years of life in the godown stole Nuraeni's youth and charm, and the young woman she had been rarely resurfaced. Her cold, catty attitude deepened when Komar asked for her wedding ring so he could buy House 131. She had to hide behind a veil when the family moved, to hide her sadness.

Their new home triggered a change in Nuraeni. She started to talk a lot, and the words sprang from dissatisfaction and unhappiness. The problem was that the words weren't directed at anyone, but to her stove and pan, her constant companions since the day of her marriage. The stove was full of rust, its flames flaring up to different heights, while the holes for the wicks were really a mess. The pan, too, had been riddled with holes until a traveling welder patched it up. She muttered dismally to the stove and pan at all hours of the day. She was particularly vituperative about the warped wicker sidings, saying they were no better than a cow shed.

Komar took the hint, and one day, after a year of living at 131, he bought rolls of new wickerwork, and with Margio's help removed and replaced the old walls. They worked hard for a week, cutting and pegging, securing them with small wedges and painting them with lime. The house was brighter after that, thanks to their work, but it didn't touch Nuraeni one bit. Sure enough, before long a storm roared through the cacao plantation and lashed the new sidings, and with the changing seasons they twisted into shapes reminiscent of a storm-lashed sea. The lime paint cracked and fell in flakes on the ground, and all of this was related bitterly by Nuraeni to her stove and pan.

There were other issues, of course. Despite Komar's repairs on the first day at the new home, many of the old roof tiles had cracked, opening a number of leaks. If Nuraeni didn't furnish the middle room with pails and bowls, the dirt floor turned to mud. Komar had to go to the brick factory for new tiles, which meant a whole day of work lost. This took care of the mud problem for a while, but when the rainy season returned, more tiles cracked and the pails and bowls reappeared. In the company of the stove and the pan, Nuraeni mocked herself.

Komar could never make the house as nice as the ones lining the side of the big road, and he knew it. To shut her nagging mouth, which always found cause for complaint, Komar had a ready excuse. "There's not much we can do as long as Ma Rabiah still owns the land."

Yet later, when they did own the land, little improved, and Nuraeni kept up her conversations with the kitchenware. Komar began to think his wife had gone mad, but he never let that thought deter him when it came to plundering her flesh.

Four

Margio seldom saw his mother happy, and often thought of doing things to cheer her up. He would go back to their kampong and look for gifts for her. If he had some money from doing odd jobs at other people's houses, Margio would buy his mother ten sticks of satay or a new pair of flip-flops, which lifted the gloom for a little while. Nothing worked for long, and when he realized that he started to direct his frustration at Komar.

Back then, Komar often hit Nuraeni right in front of their son, beating her black and blue. Margio was still too small to intervene, and he often got whacked himself. He would lean against the door, with Mameh at his side biting the hem of her dress, while Nuraeni cowered in a corner and Komar stood above her with the rattan duster in his hand. Komar always found some excuse to swing it at her.

Sometimes the beatings happened outdoors, and Nuraeni would run round the house for all the neighbors to see. Komar chased her, and devils orbiting them stoked his anger, until Nuraeni ran into the house to shield herself with the door. But Komar always pushed his way in, on one occasion shivering the door to pieces. He would throw her to the floor and kick her thighs over and over. The watching neighbors would rub their chests, and Margio turned his face away. Mameh was the only one who cried, sobbing for a long time afterward in her mother's embrace.

His mother's stubbornness began to manifest in Margio, who wouldn't fight Komar but took to provoking him, goading him to swing the rattan cane. Sometimes Komar didn't like it when Margio left for his grandfather's kampong, but the boy stood his ground. On a Saturday afternoon, he'd leave without saying a word, returning on Sunday night to face Komar's rage. The next day Margio would limp to school, after Komar had beat him, plunged him into the water tub, yanked at his ears and thrown a coconut shell dipper at him. Komar would often feel envious when he watched the boy calmly playing with his marbles, trading cards, and crickets. Margio would grow more unyielding to Komar's grumbling, chipping away at the man's patience until he got smacked. Margio never fought back, as everyone knew, but stayed calm with his toys until Komar seized them and threw them into the trash. Margio would pull them back out, and Komar would run after him, dragging him along by one of his feet, with the boy's sprawled body scraping against the ground. Margio would be lifted and tossed into the house, smashing against a chair leg. The boy would simply grimace, and the unsatisfied Komar would come after him again, grabbing him by the hair and banging him against a wooden pole. On one occasion the kid's forehead gushed blood, but Margio never backed down.

Even gentle-mannered Mameh got her share of the rattan duster, the same way he'd lash out at a stray cat when it passed him. Peace came only in the idyll between Komar's departure on his bicycle to the barbershop at the market and his return.

When they finally acquired the land from Ma Rabiah, Komar decided to lay down a cement floor. It was his last effort to quiet Nuraeni, and he ordered Margio to help. Margio was then fifteen years old, a young man who had once joined Major Sadrah's boar-hunting party, and strong enough to mix the cement. They worked on Sundays. Komar mixed the cement with lime to make it stickier, while Margio turned the paste with a mortar. Nuraeni served them sweet tea, bananas, and sweet-potato fritters, but wasn't happy about Komar's big plan.

Their floor did not reveal itself in a day, but gradually emerged. First there was the living room, where planks were laid down while the cement dried. The next Sunday they covered the two bedroom floors. After four weeks the entire house had hard flooring all the way to the kitchen and even on the terrace. Mameh could sit on the floor to play board games like mancala with her friends, or roll out a mat and lounge about. Komar grew increasingly affectionate, praising Margio's work, and still Nuraeni remained cold to him, and untouched by the pretense.

Five months went by and they found a crack in the floor. At first Komar thought it must've been caused by the raw lime and was certain that it wouldn't get any worse. But the crack grew, and by the end of the month it was a kind of crater, as if a five-ton steel ball had bounced off the floor. A neighbor said it was probably caused by the damp, another told them that a trash hole or a well must have been there once. Holes emerged, one in the living room, two in the kitchen, and a small one in a bedroom.

Just as she had with the bamboo walls and the roof tiles, Nuraeni celebrated the crumbling of Komar's work by gossiping about it with the various utensils in the kitchen. After listening to this babble, Margio could only walk away, because he knew that once Komar's patience had reached its limit, he would drag Nuraeni into the bedroom and slap her, or throw her against the stove.

His home was a wild place, and Margio humbly admitted that in all his years he hadn't understood the relationship between his parents. How did two people dedicated to punishing each other come to live like this? In Komar's place, Margio wasn't sure he could bear Nuraeni's sneers and scathing whispers; and Komar was utterly contemptible. The man never hesitated to use his fists on his family, driving them closer to their graves every day. But in the end Komar gave up and yelled at Nuraeni: "Everything in this house is your responsibility!" And so it was. Komar became increasingly engrossed in raising chickens and rabbits. He had a gamecock that he would take to the cockpit, and he bred pigeons to race at the soccer field or the abandoned railway station.

After Komar stopped giving a damn, Nuraeni took more pride in the house, although Margio and Mameh soon realized she had an extremely weird idea of decor. One day she cut up some old calendars, and pinned pictures of the Taj Mahal and the actress Meriam Bellina to the wall above the wooden chairs in the living room where they received guests. She also cut up Margio's old drawing book, where she found Margio's inept drawings of mountain scenery along with some calligraphy, and put these up next to the door. No one commented, neither Margio nor Mameh. They worried that would only make her sadder, though it was plain that what she was doing didn't make her happy either.

Then one day she received an allamanda seedling from an old neighbor. The yard had always been totally bare, a place for children to play marbles, but now she planted the seedling there. Margio was glad she had something to keep her occupied, no matter how trivial, though he had lost his spot to play marbles. Every morning Nuraeni watered her plant, and by the time it started to look firm and the leaves were no longer drooping, she got a bundle of golden dewdrop seedlings. She turned them into a living fence around the front yard, leaving a narrow space through which people could walk into the house. She watered the golden dewdrops, and Mameh sometimes thought she seemed more interested in the care of her plants than in that of her children.

One by one other flowering plants arrived, while the allamanda and the golden dewdrops grew sturdier and greener. She planted jasmine by the kitchen wall, roses in four groups near the golden dewdrops, and then came the mussaenda. Globe amaranths thrived alongside the ditch flanking one side of the house. Lantana shrubs grew next to the terrace's disintegrating wall. Wild lilies bloomed near the garbage hole, and from the tall old allamanda she took seeds and planted them in the eastern corner of the yard. They had most extensive flower garden in the entire town, putting any flowershop to shame, because Nuraeni grew even the achiote, together with the saka siri, both of which required a great deal of moisture in the soil. The coastal morning glory was left to creep up a bamboo pole that leaned against the kapok tree.

Further plantings came in the form of hibiscus and jungle

111

flame, which seemed to bring density to the limited space of the yard, together with the bougainvillea whose seeds Margio brought home from school. Last were several orchids planted in coconut shells and hung from the house's rafters. Komar watched the spread of flowers with awe, thinking his wife was beautifying their house, and hoping it would improve her attitude. The plants became lush with the arrival of the monsoon season, and some began to bud. Colors appeared amid the jungle of green, and like his father, Margio spied on Nuraeni, hoping to see her cheerful at the luxuriant growth in her garden.

It turned out the plants were *too* healthy. The yard, which they had imagined a beautiful garden adorning their little house, was now a jungle, with blooms popping up every which way. Months passed and the allamanda began to soar, its highest tips slithering over the roof, its bright yellow flowers contrasting sharply with the blue sky, enchanting butterflies. The jasmine by the kitchen wall was a glimmer of white against a dark-green background, like stars in a night sky. Everything spread rapidly, like the dense golden dewdrops that had grown into a solid fence.

The garden became indistinguishable from dense undergrowth, and Margio started to call it a wilderness. The leaves either withered or jostled each other for light. Komar realized his assumptions about what Nuraeni was doing were quite wrong, and he treated the plants with his old disgust. Returning from the barbershop, he'd let the wheels of his bicycle squash some golden dewdrops, or hurl the bike onto a rose bush. The mistreatment killed some of the plants, and others withered, adding to the chaos. Within two years, no one could see the façade of the house; it was covered entirely

112

by shimmering green leaves. When guests came, they had to ask where the front door was. Dead plants fertilized the soil, and the remainder thrived.

One day Mameh saw a snake slithering over the terrace and screamed until Margio caught it. It was a small, common tree snake, a venomless and quite harmless kind. Kids would play with them, letting them glide in and out of their fingers, and magicians managed to slide them into one nostril and out the other. But it made Mameh think about chopping down Nuraeni's flowers, or at least returning the yard to the beautiful garden it once was, with slender, well-trimmed trees. She was all set with a machete and a stick, but Nuraeni caught her, and said to her firmly, "No!" Mameh didn't dare argue, for the expression on her mother's face said she wouldn't tolerate anyone touching her wilderness. Mameh gave up and put the machete and stick back in the kitchen.

Only later did Mameh understand what her mother was up to. Nuraeni hoped to make the house as ugly as possible, as much a ruin as she had said it would be on the first day they arrived. Such a depth of bitterness expressed in this ironic manner, as she spoiled the house with flowers, scared Mameh.

She never tried to touch the plants again. No matter how much she wanted to pick the brilliant jasmines or the blood-red roses, she always held back for fear of her mother. Mameh had never seen Nuraeni furious before, anger being Komar's privilege—not until she tried to touch the flowers. It frightened her. She thought that if Nuraeni really lost her temper, the results would be far worse than her husband's everyday brutality.

The flower jungle became more than a nest for snakes and caterpillars; it was a hideout for foxes and thieves. The neighbors did laugh about it now, and Komar continued to crush the flowers. If someone asked what the flowers were for, Nuraeni was quick to reply: "For my funeral."

Only once did Mameh see Nuraeni plucking flowers, not long after Marian died. She was singing strange ballads, which Mameh didn't recognize. Perhaps they dated back to the time when her mother was still a girl. These melancholy songs flowed, while her fingers tweaked each flower carefully and placed it in her basket. It was as if plucking the flowers were the same as killing them, and her sorrow for them as great as the void left by the baby.

When Komar bin Syueb died, Mameh followed her mother's example by picking flowers for the burial. At first she thought her mother would let her do it, because so little had been given to the dead man, but the look on her face made it clear that Nuraeni disapproved. She had given too much to that bastard already. But Mameh was now a young woman, and didn't always obey her mother's wishes. She kept picking flowers, regardless of her mother's pain.

By this time Margio had concluded that nothing would ever make Nuraeni happy. Certainly not the flowers. As long as they reigned over the yard, turning it into a crazy jungle, Nuraeni's nonsense chats with the stove and pan were unstoppable, a symptom of a grief that never left her. But even if the flower jungle didn't make her happy, it gave her some kind of solace, and for that small blessing, the normally careless Margio was always extra careful around the plants. Nothing else came close to lifting his mother's mood.

Until one day after he had stayed up really late watching a *wayang* performance about the death of Semar, the mysterious and powerful pariah god. He had come home to get

114

something to eat that morning, after briefly sleeping at the nightwatch hut, and he found his mother beaming. He had never seen her like this. There was color in her cheeks. Her round eyes were brighter and, look, she had lipstick on, and face powder, and looked washed and fresh, too.

Warm rice, bawal fish, and coconut and vegetable soup were set out on the dining table. It wasn't often that his mother started so early. He had only expected to find last night's leftovers, and was amazed by the sudden change at home. He whispered Mameh to ask if something had happened, but she was just as baffled, despite being home so much. They checked the calendar and the *Weton* list of holidays, but it was just an ordinary day. They gave up and assumed that her good mood wouldn't last beyond sundown, but they were wrong. Nuraeni became happier every day, despite retaining every ounce of bitterness toward Komar.

With time, her belly gave her away, and Margio realized what was really going on. Nuraeni was pregnant. He also had a feeling that the baby was a girl because, as people said, that's how it is when a woman suddenly becomes exceptionally beautiful during pregnancy. Popular wisdom would be proved right when Marian was born.

Nuraeni craved odd foods, like raw cacao, and Margio roamed all over the bankrupt plantation looking for a tree that still bore fruit. On another occasion she asked for banana-heart soup, and it was Mameh who cooked it for her.

In truth their mother's pregnancy irked Margio and Mameh. Think about it, said Margio to his sister. He was almost twenty years old, and now suddenly he was about to have a raw, red baby sibling. But the radiance of his mother's face persuaded Margio to be extra-attentive. He worried she might be too old to bear a child safely. How old was she now? Margio calculated she was at least thirty-eight. Still fairly young, and the twinkle in her eyes had restored some of her youth. She could still get pregnant two or three times more, thought the boy.

Nuraeni's behavior toward Komar didn't change. He saw her talking to the stove and the pan still, and although now her tone was cheerful and teasing, his indifference to her was so great he didn't notice anything unusual. He was the last to find out.

For a long time, she had been going to Anwar Sadat's home to help with housework, and she didn't stop until the birth. Komar allowed her to help at Anwar Sadat's because there was so little to do at home. Major Sadrah's wife would often ask Nuraeni to cook when her children visited or military guests came to dinner, and she would be allowed to take some of the food back with her. She worked in a shop cooking and making cakes, too. But where she worked most often was at Anwar Sadat's place, which was next-door. Kasia had to go to the hospital every day, and was always busy when she got home. Her daughters meanwhile were nothing more than parasites. Nuraeni would help by cooking rice and vegetable dishes. She'd wash and iron their laundry, sweep the floor and the yard, and take care of Maesa Dewi' little baby.

Every day, after Komar had his breakfast and pedaled his bicycle to the shade of the tropical almond tree in the market, Nuraeni would hurry to Kasia's house and enter without even knocking, first to bathe the little baby, then to carry dirty clothes to the bathroom while Maesa Dewi and Laila lay sprawled on the couch, munching potato chips, and Anwar Sadat swayed in his rocking chair, smoking a clove

116

cigarette. Nuraeni would then cook lunch while the dirty clothes were soaking in soapy water. Being pregnant didn't stop her doing all these chores, and that was one reason why Komar didn't realize they were about to have a third child.

Actually, Margio was the first in the family to hang out at Anwar Sadat's house, where he was often asked to do odd jobs. It began when he had just moved to number 131. Margio was told by his father to learn to read the Koran under the supervision of Ma Soma. These classes were a sweet excuse for Margio to escape his boring house and offered a place to make new friends. He also discovered another attraction.

After the Isha prayers, he'd huddle with some of the other kids on Anwar Sadat's front terrace, beside the large windows. There were no televisions in most local homes, but Sadat had one and let Margio and the others watch it. Sometimes older men, puffing clouds of tobacco smoke, would also come to watch the television, seated on coconut-wood chairs lined up on the terrace. The little kids were timid about going inside, because there, in front of the television set, the family would be sitting quiet and unperturbed, with the girls munching green peas. It wasn't proper to disturb such tranquillity, so peeping through the windows was as close as they got.

On certain occasions, however, Anwar Sadat would let them in. In a commanding tone, he would tell them to sit on a braided mat, which took the place of chairs, or on the sofa. Sometimes they listened to him, except when they had chores to do. However, they would definitely comply when there were signs that Anwar Sadat was going to show a video. The man often went to a video rental shop in the hotel by the beach, especially on Saturday nights, and would let the

117

children from the surau watch. This was how Margio became as familiar with *Kungfu Shaolin* as he was with *Rambo*.

One evening Margio sat alone outside Anwar Sadat's window. It was raining heavily, so the other kids had run home, but not Margio. All that afternoon Komar had been beating Nuraeni, and he didn't want to see it going on into the night. He planned to start his evening watching television and conclude it by sleeping at the surau. Anwar Sadat's family shot the breeze until one of them complained about being hungry, and Margio understood they hadn't prepared anything for supper. Seeing Margio sitting on the terrace, Anwar Sadat approached him and asked if he was willing to go buy food at the market. Although it was late, there would usually still be vendors around, offering fried tempeh, chicken satay, and even grilled fish. Before Margio could say yes, Maharani, the youngest daughter, stepped out of the house and told her father she would go, too. They shared an umbrella, braving the rain and the dark.

That was how Margio started doing odd jobs for Anwar Sadat and, more important, the beginning of his magical relationship with Maharani. They were the same age.

As Anwar Sadat had no son and was the only male in the house, every time he faced a job that was physically demanding he would go to number 131 and ask Margio for help. Margio could carry sacks of rice to the storeroom, fix a leaking roof gutter, and chop back shrubs in the house's front yard. For these chores Anwar Sadat gave him money, or even asked him to dine with them, and on Lebaran gave him new pants and shoes. Finally one day Anwar Sadat asked if he could call his mother to help cook, and so he fetched Nuraeni.

And so Anwar Sadat offered a means of escape to another

member of the family, freeing Nuraeni from a home life that was beyond repair. Even if Kasia didn't pay her, she liked going to Anwar Sadat's place, no matter how much work needed doing there. A bowl of soup and a few slices of meat was enough. At Anwar Sadat's she could listen to the sad songs he played from his office and enjoy the sight of his beautiful, self-indulgent daughters. She was never annoyed with these girls, especially Laila and Maesa Dewi, no matter what they asked her to do. Laila would repeatedly request a massage and Maesa Dewi would want some noodles, and Nuraeni would comply with pleasure. In this house Nuraeni never talked to the stove; she recovered some of her former sweetness.

With time, these chores became such a part of her routine that Anwar Sadat and Kasia had no need to call for her any more. Instead she appeared all of a sudden as though having fallen through the ceiling, sometimes at dawn, and ask if Kasia wanted help with cooking that morning. Kasia normally ruled the kitchen at breakfast time, but if she felt lazy she would happily hand over to Nuraeni.

Taking as much pride in the house as if it were hers, Nuraeni would polish the floor to a shine the real owner could never equal, rubbing each tile's edges with a small rag to make sure that not a single spot of dust was overlooked, rubbing it like a cat licking its paws. She'd make the windowpanes vanish into absolute transparency, fooling the bugs and moths, which slammed against them. She had never done this at number 131 with their two windowpanes, which had been dulled by lime splatters when Komar and Margio were whitewashing the walls. Nuraeni wouldn't let the flowers in the yard wilt either, quite unlike her own flower jungle, and this added to Kasia's delight. She kept Nuraeni on, as if she owned a loyal servant willing to work even without a penny's pay.

The attractions of this home from home grew with the gentleness that greeted her there, in stark contrast to Komar's brutality. It was plain he knew Nuraeni was happy in this house, and he was jealous. On her return he would punish her with all the usual atrocities, lashing out with the rattan duster and raping her come evening. He treated her body with increasing contempt. But he could never stop her from going, since he had to go to work. And when he learned that Anwar Sadat and Kasia gave Nuraeni and Margio far more money than he had ever managed to make, he understood that his power over her was waning. He couldn't stop them. He could only respond to their kindness by being odious.

In the end, danger came from another quarter entirely. The fine treatment Nuraeni received teased and stirred her until she lost her common sense. It wasn't her near-selfless devotion that undermined her, something she offered sincerely in return for the rare gift of kindness. It was Anwar Sadat's womanizing nature, moved by the remains of her youthful beauty—an attraction his own wife had never possessed.

One day, when Nuraeni was slicing onions, standing at a table next to a stove humming with boiling water, Anwar Sadat walked by and pinched her behind. She was stunned. She had heard the gossip about this man, a wolf who couldn't keep his hands to himself, and as she turned to stare him down, her round eyes widened. But what she saw wasn't lust, but an innocent smile on a gentle face, like the face of a small

120

child. She just couldn't get angry. Confronted with such a sweet expression, she could only shoo him away, saying it wasn't proper, especially if his one of his daughters were to see.

His girls made themselves scarce when she was there. Laila often went out and Maesa Dewi preferred to stay in bed. Since Nuraeni hadn't got angry with him, Anwar Sadat developed a habit of pinching her buttocks or patting them whenever the opportunity arose. Nuraeni no longer turned her head with widened eyes, but blushed instead, her lips forming a constrained smile that was hard to decipher. The touch felt friendly to her, the kind of attention she had not experienced before. She flushed perhaps because she liked it, though she saw the rudeness as well. And every time the man appeared, striding in with a suggestive smile, she felt her bosom tingle and waited in trepidation for his hand to reach for her.

One day Anwar Sadat did more than just pinch her buttocks, as if he were testing fruit, but stopped behind Nuraeni while she stood separating the caterpillar-chewed leaves from a bunch of spinach. This time she felt his breath on her hair and the nape of her neck. She was flooded with a terror that froze her body, while Anwar Sadat's hand clung to her dress, gripping her behind. She wondered what he was going to do, and how she should react. Anwar Sadat slowly pushed his body onto hers, lightly pressing Nuraeni against the table. She didn't have the courage to turn her head, because if she did that they would be looking into each other's eyes, face to face, their noses touching. Nuraeni trembled, her icy hands hanging down, while the spinach stems scattered across the table. Anwar Sadat leaned on her back, pushing against her buttocks. One hand loosened its tight grip; the other felt her breasts with a soft touch that made her tingle warmly, until the back-and-forth rubbing entered her every cell. Nuraeni caught her breath as his hands moved over her.

She went limp, unresisting. Anwar Sadat, realizing that her body was his, moved his hands downward, pressing her dress's fabric onto her skin before slowly pulling it up to stroke her plump thighs. Once the dress was lifted and its hem hooked on his index finger, his hand slid in without rushing, and the contact made the hair on her skin stand on end. He moved his fingers up, down, and around. Suddenly, she came to her senses. Ice entered her veins, and her body jolted with alarm.

She straightened her dress, brushing Anwar Sadat's hands away. She lightly nudged the man off her back with her elbows. Her rejection was gentle, ambiguous almost, and Anwar Sadat took the opportunity to caress her buttocks once more. Then he retreated, accepting that his time had not yet come. By all accounts, he was a great lover.

Nuraeni turned around, the redness on her cheeks spreading. The blush didn't suggest anger so much as coyness. Anwar Sadat simply smiled and slipped on his innocent mask, before walking away and letting her resume her role as the perfect mistress of his kitchen.

After that, Nuraeni worked fast and went home early with a bowl of spinach soup. She stayed away from Anwar Sadat's house, but on the second day Kasia came to check on her. Nuraeni pretended she was ill. She really was feeling unwell, because time and again her body would tremble when she remembered that body pressing in on hers, and that hand skimming over the skin at the top of her thighs, almost

122

penetrating her most secret places. The encounter kept coming back to her, and she could still feel his caresses, sometimes warm and sometimes cold. The more she tried, the harder it was to forget.

After three days, she managed to overcome the fever. She could remember what happened without the horror and pain, and began to see its startling, intimate side—its unfamiliar warmth. Despite a sneaking shame, Nuraeni missed him and longed for that touch of his on her behind, for it to creep farther in and reach inside her. And so she returned, apprehensive this time, holding back for a moment at the door, like a first-time guest, and entered the kitchen to work, though her thoughts fluttered distractedly. She heard someone approach and recognized his footsteps from the way he dragged his slippers. There was no need to turn around to understand that Anwar Sadat was creeping toward her. Even so, she looked. He was dressed only in underpants and a shirt with the top button undone, smiling in a way no longer guileless, but filled with intent. Nuraeni was bashful in response, smiling shyly, lowering her head while her eyes remained riveted on the approaching figure. Anwar Sadat understood that this woman had been conquered, and he was coming to get her.

Again he stood behind her with his arms circling her body, restraining her and seeming to silence everything. It was as if the air were solidifying around her. She was cornered, but aware that she appeared to be giving consent and afraid of what that might mean and whether he would be rough with her. She felt his face sink into her hair, warmly moving down to the nape of her neck. She heard the panting sound of his breath, its rhythm out of sync with the explosion of her own gasps. He moved his hands to pinch her pelvis between his fingers, controlling her hips.

They swayed together, finding a kind of rhythm in the silent kitchen. For the moment, they were like cuddling new-lyweds. Anwar Sadat's hands slid over her slowly, very slowly, building up the tension gradually, because he knew that rashness would ruin all. His fingers were above her waist, going upward. His palms cupped Nuraeni's breasts, caressing them. Her breasts, which had aged and suckled children, which had been punished at Komar's hands, were firmer in the steaming air of the kitchen, under Anwar Sadat's hot fingers. Youth blossomed again under her flesh.

Anwar Sadat realized that if only he'd gotten his hands on this woman years ago, he would have discovered an almost perfect physique. For months she had been coming to his house, and he had watched her, and he regretted every minute he had delayed approaching her. Throughout those months he had scrutinized her beauty, discerned it beneath the sadness, despite her silence and her morbid preoccupation with housework. Never before had he so much as flirted with a close neighbor, a woman he knew well, the wife of a friend, and above all a woman who could roam about his house like a sister-in-law. But her misty look, and his ability to intuit what she had suffered, made her too compelling for him to back away. He was bewitched by the idea that she longed for the touch of a great lover, something he felt he could slowly provide to this disap-pointed woman.

He felt he was weighing up her suffering as he held her breasts and listened to the breath catch in her throat. He could understand her condition, yet continued to be awed.

She had preserved her body despite everything. He could feel her desire, her breasts seemed to grow firmer, as if to prove his assumption that this woman needed this kind of touch, his touch, to bring her to life.

He would give her the warmth she pined for. His practiced hands, which had fashioned the naturalistic statues in front of his house, which had sloshed paint in shameless imitation of Raden Saleh's art, and had sent numerous women into raptures under his body, began to move swiftly, fingers lifting before sinking in, drawing patterns on her skin. Sure enough, Nuraeni began to press herself against him, gazing at the ceiling with empty eyes, and breathing heavily through parted lips. Anwar Sadat gripped her more firmly, tightened his cupped hands, and rotated his palms as if opening a jar. Once or twice, all this sent them ramming against each other, as their minds emptied, their legs began to give way, and their bodies were soaked with sweat. Nuraeni's dress fastened with two buttons at the neck. Anwar Sadat's hand slowly unbuttoned them, three fingers working as if they had eyes, before his hands slid into her dress and into the bra.

They were rapt, growing wilder with each breath, when a door opened somewhere at the front of the house, bringing their passion to a halt. When Maesa Dewi entered the kitchen, Nuraeni was facing the table holding a knife, with nothing before her to slice, just standing there without the courage to turn around, for Maesa Dewi might see the wide-open collar of her dress revealing her bra. Meanwhile Anwar Sadat was by the teapot, pouring water into a glass before drinking it, also not turning around. Something in his shorts quickly wilted. For a moment, Maesa stared at them both, before dashing into the bathroom and pissing loudly. Anwar Sadat left the kitchen without a word being said.

Basically, had Margio and Mameh been really alert, they would have dated the change in their mother to that day. She glowed that evening, and the look in her eye was something that had been absent since the days of her girlhood. She bathed for hours, put on her prettiest dress, bought four years ago for Lebaran, and played with the kitten by the stove as the rice cooked. She didn't normally pay attention to pets, but she stroked the cat's fur, letting her fingers be nibbled, singing softly as if lulling it to sleep. Mameh noticed this, Margio witnessed it, and later Komar stared in disbelief, but they all took it simply for another form of insanity.

Nuraeni mulled over what happened that afternoon. For her there was nothing more beautiful, and she missed Anwar Sadat's touch very much. She could think of nothing but the memory of that moment and what awaited them, because she sensed it wasn't over yet; there was more to come.

She walked to Anwar Sadat's house at ten the next morning, shivering with anticipation. She wore a blouse with a row of five buttons and a flouncy skirt, a gesture of sur-render, giving Anwar Sadat easy access. She wanted to repeat what they had done yesterday, and her heart beat fast, but she worried that Maesa Dewi might prove to be a snooping demon. She entered the house, treading softly on the tiles, and headed for the kitchen making a great pretence of inno-cence. She kept her eyes fixed on the space ahead of her while her mind roved the house, hoping for some sign of his pres-ence. She stood in the middle of the kitchen, the stove on one side, the table and cupboard crammed together on the other.

She stood between them, without wanting to touch anything, not the wok nor the pan, not the knife nor the potatoes. There she was, waiting for his hands on her body.

She heard the door open. Nuraeni stood still, and didn't look. But once again she recognized the dragging of his feet, the man she was waiting for. Upon seeing the helpless woman in the center of his kitchen, Anwar Sadat knew that the afternoon was theirs. She was telling him, without words, to do as he liked, to meld them together.

He took her hand and, with shuffling steps, led her to the bedroom. He closed the door and locked them inside. A truly intimate realm, it was now inaccessible to anyone else, even Maesa Dewi and Kasia.

Anwar Sadat remained stood by the door, taking in Nuraeni in all her bashfulness. Her head was bowed; she didn't know where to look. She moved backward until she bumped against the edge of the bed and fell onto the mattress. Her hands touched the sheet, which was was lily-white, soft, and thick, with the motif of a hummingbird reapeated in dark brown thread. The foam mattress underneath was solid and yet supple. She wanted to find a warm, eternal sleep, with no wife-beater to bully her and no worries. Anwar Sadat walked toward her. She watched his legs move, and her daydreaming stopped as she looked up at the innocent face of her conqueror.

They exchanged a brief look, and Nuraeni smiled shyly as she glanced at his bulging briefs. It made her freeze again, but Anwar Sadat touched her shoulder, bringing the warmth back to her skin. She sprawled there, legs dangling to the floor, her hair spilling out abundantly, and her breasts shaken by her heavy breathing. Anwar Sadat spread her legs and stood between them before throwing himself down, pressing himself onto her body. The heaviness was thrilling, and stirring, as if saying to her that this could not be delayed any longer.

It was clear from the first that Anwar Sadat would be a patient, attentive lover. He buried his lips in hers, while his hands circled her waist, not letting her escape. Nuraeni was stiff at first, letting their dry lips touch, disorientated by not being able to see him as he lay on top of her. But she could feel the man's mouth gulping like a fish at the surface of a pond, sending a wet current through her parted lips. He kept teasing her to respond, biting her lower lip and pulling at it slightly, and letting it go before kissing it fully. A response finally came, in tiny movements, until suddenly she was kissing him hard in return.

After that everything became easier. Anwar Sadat took in the scent of her neck, his face moving along hers, kissing the back of one ear, then the other, and again finding her lips. As they writhed together, Nuraeni pushed herself up with her feet, getting her legs, which had sprawled over the side of the mattress, properly onto the bed.

They didn't lose all restraint, but slowed down, like lovers who understood the art of lovemaking. Anwar Sadat undid the five buttons of her blouse so gently and unconsciously that when everything was laid open neither of them were aware of it. She was half-naked now, and Anwar Sadat sat over her thighs and took off his undershirt to expose a chest thick with salt-and-pepper hair. The two of them stared at each other, until Anwar Sadat placed his palms on her breasts and poured lustful kisses onto Nuraeni's lips without loosening his hold. Her skirt and his underpants slipped away without their bodies separating, undone by the skilful hands that threw them to the floor. Now they were completely naked, with Nuraeni's knees lifted and her legs looped around his body. They took their time to make love there, sweating and gasping on top of the crumpled hummingbird sheet.

The moment was so profound for them, it would be almost impossible to remember. Lying naked they said nothing, shorn of anything to talk about, for desire apparently needed no words. With bodies and souls worn out, they lay side by side, their half-extinguished eyes fixed on the ceiling. The only light came through the thin curtain covering the window, as the sun soared toward noon. Nuraeni was still astonished by the boldness of her own body, and unspeakably elated. There was no need to ask the man how he felt. Finally with no hesitation, the woman turned aside, resting her thigh on Anwar Sadat's body, and closed her eyes, smiling slightly.

That afternoon Nuraeni came home and no one was conscious of a change in her behavior. Perhaps she hid her joy too well, or the other inhabitants simply paid her too little attention. Anwar Sadat alone saw it, captivated by how he'd been able to make a fresh newlywed out of this woman; and he continued to make himself available to her as their days grew hotter and wilder, in the same bed and occasionally in other places. There were times when Maesa Dewi would go out, and together they would close the doors and curtains, dim the lights, and fuck on the sofa and on the kitchen table, inside the water tub, and once on the floor of his studio.

When she became pregnant, Nuraeni didn't need a midwife or a doctor to tell her the news. She could feel the change. She didn't panic at all. In fact she was overjoyed and would sit in contemplation of the future-born, stroking a belly that was not yet protruding, as if this were the only true child she would ever have. It was as if it were her long-awaited firstborn, and she would be filled with tears anticipating the day she would bring it into the world, to hear its cry, to see it grow, and she knew she would love it. She often chanted softly, as if the child were born and she were already soothing its little pains.

It was then that Margio began to sense the change in his mother. She was better dressed, more lively, and prettier than he had ever seen her. Much later on, he would realize that the glow originated with a baby girl nestled in her womb. He whispered to Mameh that their mother was pregnant, and both were awed as they waited for the unexpected baby. At the time Margio still thought the baby was his father's, although he did wonder how Komar had managed it. For years, probably since the flower jungle came to be, Nuraeni had slept in Mameh's room, and considering his aging body, and the complaint he once made about a swelling on his organ, Margio was surprised to learn Komar could conceive a child.

Margio imagined how one night Komar would have dragged Nuraeni from Mameh's room and thrown her into bed or over the chest in the rice storage room and had his cruel way with her. He must've done it over and over to get his beleaguered wife pregnant again, which he had done regardless of the fact the two existing children were generally underfed. He didn't talk about this with his sister, he kept his doubts to himself, and became surprised that after Nuraeni's belly looked rounder and rounder, Komar didn't seem to notice. Not a word was said about a baby sibling, and he paid no special attention to his wife.

When Komar bin Syueb finally found out she was pregnant, his rage was out of control. The violence stunned both Margio and Mameh, because Komar had been ignoring his wife for so long, even though he would still beat her up at times, and his violence had ebbed. But this storm was more brutal than anything they had witnessed in a long time, a suppressed rage bursting forth. He dragged her from the kitchen to the center of the house, and slapped her without saying a word. Nuraeni screamed in anger, as if the woman wanted to fight back now after all, perhaps to defend the beloved child in her womb. She called him a beast, a devil, a swine, and Komar replied in kind. Seeing how Nuraeni fought back, Komar became more aggressive still. No longer using the palms of his hands, he hit her with his fists, punching her in the forehead.

Nuraeni was flung against the wall, making the flimsy bamboo siding wobble. Komar came after her, swinging his foot into her calves. Cornered, Nuraeni crashed to the floor. While she lay prone, he kicked her in the hips as well until Nuraeni caught his foot. Revolted by the sight of a woman who would not accept defeat, Komar grabbed her by the hair, hauling the grimacing Nuraeni up onto her toes. As they stood eye to eye, Komar smacked her in the jaw, and this time she staggered to another corner, her face red and raw. She still refused to shed a tear, defending her belly with her hands while he pummelled her.

"You whore!" shrilled Komar, as he threw a tin ashtray at her head and walked away.

Margio and Mameh watched, ashen-faced and horrified.

131

By the time they had recovered enough to do something, Komar had left. Mameh approached her mother, propped her up, and guided her to the mattress. Mameh had always been the quiet child, slow to cry, but at the sight of her battered mother she broke into choking sobs, fanning Nuraeni, caressing her bruises, and inquiring after her needs—did she want a sponge? A cold compress?—while the tears flowed. Nuraeni just shook her head and clutched at her daughter's hands.

Now Margio understood that the unborn baby wasn't Komar's. His father's incandescent rage had lit up the truth, and for a moment the boy didn't know which side to take. It was almost impossible to believe that Nuraeni had conceived a child with another man. He couldn't think who that other man could be.

The shame he felt was visceral. He wanted to retch and staggered away from home to the nightwatch hut, where he continued to mull over all that had happened. No matter where his mind wandered, there was no escape from the stark, stubborn reality. He couldn't talk to his friends about it, even though some of them asked why he looked so miserable. There was no way he could discuss the matter. If he told his friends, soon everyone in the world would know that his mother had been impregnated by someone other than his father. One part of him wanted to see his damn parents burn. They had conspired to torture him and Mameh. But deep down he couldn't condemn his mother after all she had endured, and he couldn't curse a father who had been so grossly betrayed.

For Komar bin Syueb himself, there was nothing more agonizing than what was flaunted right in front of him, a wife pregnant with another man's child, parading in public. It threw into shadow the nagging realization that he had made his family suffer for years. At the barbershop, he worked in distracted silence. He nearly sliced off a customer's ear, and left another's hair a tattered mess. His eyes grew teary with self-pity, as he recalled all the despair-ridden years and tried to trace his mistakes to their origin.

The years had gone by so quickly, life receding in the distance like a train narrowly missed. He recalled his weary youth, when he wandered from one hamlet to another, looking for work in the factories. He would stay at each one for a few months, cutting shoe leather, carrying wheat sacks. After years of this, he found himself ill and penniless. He resorted to his shaving equipment and looked for a shady place under a tree to wait for customers and shave their heads, though he knew he couldn't make much money that way. When Syueb told him to come home to marry, his only possession of note was a thin gold wedding band, an object he never should have bragged about.

The day of the wedding arrived, and he could see how unenthusiastic his bride was. He had never written the letter she had pined for, and never apologized. It wasn't that he didn't want to write nonsense on a pink sheet of paper scented with talc, but rather that he truly didn't know what to write about. There was nothing interesting about a life under the shade of a tree waiting for customers worried about their unsightly hair. But the woman is mine, he thought. Marriage makes her mine, and she is meant for me. If she isn't there for me when I want her, I have a right to be angry.

Sitting in the barber's chair, Komar wiped his eyes with a calico cloth, worried that someone from the chicken noodle kiosk might catch him blubbing. Again he bemoaned the passage of time, gone so fast he never had a chance. He stared aghast at his hands, which had hurt his wife hundreds of times, their children too, and again his eyes brimmed with tears. The mistakes were all his. He had carved out his own sorry life for himself. But when he thought of the many times he had returned home to a gloomy wife, to the little devils he had conceived with her, it was clear to him that no man could have done much better. His family ought to have seen how blighted his life was and helped him. Since that wasn't going to happen, they should forgive his outbursts.

A man came by and asked him to cut the hair of a little boy, and Komar had to turn his face away to hide his red-rimmed eyes. He invited the child to sit in the chair. As he prepared to get to work, he tried to reconcile himself to the central new fact of his existence: Nuraeni would give birth to a baby that wasn't his.

For a while, fleetingly, he was ready to surrender to the cosmos and his own tragic fate within it. But when he got home, he had to contend with the sight of his wife's belly, and all sense of balance was lost. His temper flared and he beat her, calling her a whore, smacking her with the water-dipper, lashing her with the rattan duster. His heart only lightened when he saw his wife kneeling in a corner of the house in surrender. Then Komar went to his room and lay down alone. When night fell and brought release in the darkness, he cried without a sound, praying that the angels might descend and write down all his misfortunes in a miraculous act of holy pity.

The unborn child grew undeterred within Nuraeni's shaken womb, enduring the lashes that fell upon its mother, and perhaps developing some sense of the stepfather out there bent on preventing its birth. Mameh was always right beside her mother, now bedridden and frail, shrunk from the constant cruelty. The daughter gave Nuraeni sponge baths, gently soaping the purple bruises before smearing her flesh with a rice and galangal liniment ground in her own mouth. Despite the pain, Nuraeni remained happier than her children had ever seen her before, which touched Margio and Mameh. They had rarely seen her smile, and now she was sharing her little joy with them, a beggar doling out a few treasured pennies. To the two children, she said softly:

"If it is born, it will come with vengeance, to kill Komar bin Syueb." Mameh sobbed, and Nuraeni's words crystallized Margio's desire to kill his father.

When Nuraeni's belly grew conspicuously large, Margio barred her from doing any more housework. He wouldn't let her go to Anwar Sadat's house or to work at home. It still shamed him to know she had been naked before someone other than his father, but Margio's spirit warmed to see the pleasure his mother took in being pregnant. He took care of the house and prepared the meals. By this point, both the children had completed high school. Margio could stay at home to protect his mother from his father, and rarely hung out with his friends. Komar himself began to find some peace of mind in accepting his ill-fated life. He no longer paid attention to the woman who carried a bastard foetus around his house, and took to spending more time inside his room. Later on, he would come home from work in the wee hours and set off early, and no one knew where he went. Perhaps he kept longer hours at his barbershop, or maybe he was ignoring his business altogether and hiding out somewhere else. Whatever the truth, his family ignored him, caring nothing about what he was up to. They were happy to have him out of sight, wishing he'd have the good sense to leave forever. A man who let his wife stray shouldn't show his face at home.

When Nuraeni stopped coming to Anwar Sadat's house, Kasia made inquiries and found out about the pregnancy. After that, she paid regular visits to check on Nuraeni's health. The bruises worried her, and she frequently arrived with bananas and milk, good food for pregnant women. Nuraeni often felt embarrassed by the midwife's kindness. Kasia did not know that the baby benefitting from her ministrations was the result of her husband's infidelity. Kasia's presence was a trial, but when she said goodbye she raised the expectant mother's spirits with a report of the baby's good health, and Nuraeni's contentment was mixed with pity.

In the seventh month Mameh bathed her mother with water and flower petals. The flowers were not plucked from the jungle garden. Mameh was still convinced her mother found joy in that botanical bedlam. She bought the blossoms from an old woman at the market, and their scent was strengthened with an aromatic oil.

While Nuraeni enjoyed the heavy aroma of the blossoms, Margio was sleeping at the nightwatch hut, curled up beside Agung Yuda. Drunk on sticky-rice arak, Margio muttered, "My mother's pregnant, and there's going to be one more neglected kid in the house." He fell asleep without a blanket, despite the sting of the chilly night air. The winds grew stronger as he slept, pummeling the collapsing cacao plantation as they blew in from the sea, but still Margio remained sprawled unconscious on the braided mat. When he woke, Jafar, a neighbor on patrol duty, was talking. His voice was urgent, but Margio, half-drunk and dizzy, couldn't comprehend what was being said. Jafar repeated himself. "Your mother's about to give birth," he said. Margio had to fetch Kasia to help with the delivery.

Margio stumbled away without a word. He took the shortcut around the surau and was soon stood in front of Anwar Sadat's house, trying to gather his wits. A terrace lamp lit the dim house and other smaller lights seeped through cracks in the door and pierced the closed curtains. It was a damn cold night and they were sure to be asleep, but someone had to take care of his mother. He walked to the door, shook his head to clear it, and rapped his knuckles on the wood. Silence. He knocked again, more loudly.

There came the sound of someone stirring, and Margio stopped knocking. The front bedroom door opened, pouring light into the living room, and then the curtains were drawn back. Behind the windowpane Laila's face appeared. As soon as she recognized the boy, she opened the door. She was wearing a nightie that made Margio rather reluctant to look at her. Sniffing the arak on Margio's breath, she asked:

"What's going on? You're drunk, and you're banging on the wrong door."

"No," Margio replied. "My mother's about to give birth."

For a moment Laila stared at him, wondering whether Margio was talking drunken nonsense. Then she left him and the open door to look for Kasia. Margio fidgeted on the terrace, blew on his palm to smell his breath and snorted again and again to try and make the odor go away.

Kasia appeared with rolls of cloth and a trunk-like kitbox,

which she had Margio carry. Without saying much, she set off in haste, Margio trailing behind. Despite her age, she kept up a fast pace. Most of the children born in that hamlet had come into the world with her assistance, and had Margio and Mameh been born there, Kasia would've been the first to hold them.

Mameh and Jafar's wife stood by Nuraeni, while she lay on her mattress groaning. Komar was not at home, which wasn't unusual. Commonly he returned only out of necessity, driven back by exhaustion and hunger. "Bastard," muttered Margio on discovering his father's absence. Kasia heard what he said and snapped at him. Bad language was completely out of place. It's no good for the little baby, she added. Margio retreated to a wooden chair in the front room, while Mameh and Jafar's wife waited by the bedroom door in case Kasia needed something or asked for help.

It had only been three days since Mameh had bathed her mother with water and flower petals. The baby was coming too early, and though it might still live, it would be better off staying put a while longer. He waited nervously, as if it was his own child. He found some clove cigarettes in his pocket, and smoked non-stop during those tense minutes, listening to Kasia's voice offering solace and encouragement, and to Nuraeni's groans as she tried to push the child into the world.

Near three in the morning, as Margio impatiently watched the clock, the baby's cries were heard. The baby won't like Komar, Margio thought, his trembling fingers throwing a cigarette into the ashtray. He wanted to get a look at the baby, despite his trepidation. He was still certain it would be a girl. Mameh and Jafar's wife hadn't moved from their post by the door. It wasn't yet time to go in. Kasia hadn't called them, though the baby's cries were slicing through the darkness. Later, Jafar's wife came out carrying the rolls of cloth, the bedsheet, and a blanket soaked with blood into the bathroom. Mameh was carrying a different bundle. A fetid smell hung in the air.

Kasia appeared at the door, disposing of her rubber gloves in a plastic bag, which she gave to Mameh to throw away, and reminded Margio to properly bury the other bundle Mameh had in her hands. Margio stood up, ready to obey, but he was held back at the bedroom door by the scene inside.

His mother lay there with the baby swaddled tight beside her, no longer crying, but feeding at its mother's breast. A very emotional scene it was, under the dim light that always came in from the neighbors' house via a cluster of wires dangling from their roof. Nuraeni was looking intently into the baby's face, stroking the hair on her delicate head.

"Look, Komar," Margio mumbled to his absent father, "her face is cursed to be very happy."

Five

Under the dim gleam of a peanut vendor's lamp, she was as beautiful as a girl painted on a Chinese porcelain vase. Her abundant hair hung very straight. It was fine, sifted in the slightest wind and dancing with her every movement. She was five foot two and slender as a stork. Her figure was girlish, and her cheerful expression made more alluring by lips that pouted with every word she uttered. As befitting her name, Maharani, queen of queens, she could conquer anyone. When she took Margio's hand in a firm grasp, he trembled and the valiant boar-vanquisher was nothing more than an adorably tongue-tied schoolboy.

People were flocking to the film screen set up in the middle of the soccer field, while across the way sat a pickup truck belonging to the herbal tonic company. A man was talking into a microphone about the properties of their tonics as the crowd waited impatiently for the film to start. Some of the townspeople gathered around the pickup, lured by prizes— umbrellas, fans, wall clocks, and, most valuable of all, an eighteen-inch television set—to buy tonics that would boost virility, tighten a woman's sexual organs, work as a diet aid, improve the appetite, cure gastritis, overcome fatigue, and so on.

Margio and his friends stood behind the peanut vendor. After months at university, Maharani had become a real city girl, but it seemed that she couldn't find a boy she liked better than Margio. She always came back for him. She was wearing a tight yellow sweater to ward off the chill, a pair of flared jeans, and flip-flops. Still holding Margio's hand, the girl coyly tugged at his arm and kissed it sweetly.

They had never held hands like that before, and Margio was fascinated by the girl's nerve. It made him feel confused and vulnerable. He couldn't even turn to look at the face he so adored, and instead stared at the silhouettes of people going back and forth like fleeting shadows on the screen. He wanted very much to join them, but the skin of his arm retained a memory of the girl's lips that distracted him. Sweat trickled down the nape of his neck. He had once gone to a brothel, with a group of friends, and when it was his turn to mount the voluptuous, middle-aged woman on the bed, Margio shivered violently, horrified rather than aroused. The way he felt now surpassed the panic he had felt then, which he only survived thanks to the prostitute's skill in stroking and slowly stiffening his desire. Now he was looking for help from anyone at all. He was hoping the girl would free him from this awkward situation, and help did come when she squeezed his hand more tightly. Margio turned and met her gaze, her sparkling face. He took it all in at once, her slender nose, curved eyelashes, and parted lips.

"Do you know that I love you?" she said.

If she weren't Anwar Sadat's daughter and the younger sister of Laila and Maesa Dewi, perhaps Margio would have been more shocked to hear her say it. Trying not to upset her, the flustered boy nodded abruptly and squeezed her hand in return. It seemed to make Maharani happy, giving Margio time to turn his attention back to the blank screen and watch the shadows with a vacant stare.

Their relationship had never been as intense as this, despite the many years they had known each other. That night when Margio had accompanied her through the rain under his umbrella, they were just kids, but even then he had felt a growing awkwardness. This girl is a kind of untouched beauty, he thought, someone who sat on her sofa watching television with a family that didn't know violence, sheltered by the warmth of her home. Meanwhile he was on the terrace sitting on a stool made from a coconut palm bole, peeking at the same television through a glass pane, with nothing to protect him from the elements. There was a wall separating them, even though it was a transparent glass wall that should have let them look at and confide in one another, yet it was impermeable. On the night he found himself walking with her under the pattering membrane of the umbrella, their shoulders touching, he had considered their closeness an unpardonable indecency. And Margio felt uncomfortable with her tonight, even after all these years.

Margio liked the girl because she possessed a natural beauty, the world's ideal of beauty. He liked her for trying to close the distance between them. The boy couldn't remember the first night that marvelous face came to occupy his imagination. He felt more and more miserable at the chasm between them. For him, the love that had suddenly emerged was a brilliant illusion too confusing to be real. Maharani, on the other hand, had been in love with him from a time before she could remember, and made increasing efforts to discover whether they really belonged together.

On that rain-washed night they were no more than two children becoming friends. Being the same age, they later found themselves going to the same school, across from the soccer field, in a building that had been there since the Dutch colonialists roamed the country, not long after the boundary-staking founders had arrived. Margio would walk to her place in the morning, and Maharani would be waiting. The two kids in their school uniforms would cross the soccer field chatting about their friends. Perhaps it was during times like this that the gods flew above them, enthusiastically spinning the cords of love. These cords could break, but for Margio and Maharani they grew stronger until the youngsters dreamed of being together, of sharing and owning each other. And when it was time to go home, Maharani would wait at the school gate, and Margio would be ready to walk side by side with her across the same green grassland.

The cords unraveled and refastened obscurely, ensnaring them, and Margio spent day after day at Anwar Sadat's house. When he needed some physical help, Anwar treated the boy like a son. The man's affection was sincere, thanks to Margio's excellent behavior. It seemed that Anwar Sadar had begun to suspect that his youngest had fallen for the boy, but he couldn't care less what kind of man his daughter chose, after all the tiresome episodes in the young lives of Laila and Maesa Dewi.

Maharani would sit on the sofa with Margio to watch the afternoon TV shows, and anyone could see they were like a couple of tamed lovers, born to be together. Since such behavior was allowed, Margio grew fonder of Anwar's home than his own. He enjoyed eating bags of chips with Maharani, but the awkwardness deep inside never faded. He continually reminded himself that the intimacy would be temporary—a brief delight. Maharani would find another man and fall in love with him and soon forget the boy named Margio. The boy always stood ready for the day when the name Maharani would be merely a sweet memory.

When Anwar Sadat sent the girl east to university, Margio told himself that this was freedom. It was better for him to see her choose another man and ignore him than to be continually tortured by the possibility of having her. He was sure there would be loads of boys at university, most of them damn smart, none of whom would fail to notice the arrival of a beautiful girl. They would compete for her, and in time Maharani would be caught. Margio was full of this dismal hope when he saw her leave, as he carried her bags. Maharani was leaving with Anwar Sadat, catching the bus outside their house, which waited next to the oil palm trees. Margio lifted the heavy bags into the trunk as Maharani kissed the hands of her mother, then Laila and Maesa Dewi, before standing before him and unexpectedly asking him for his hand. Margio let his hand be kissed, which caused his stomach to lurch. But it was nothing compared to the time when her hand suddenly gripped his arm tightly, not to ask for a goodbye kiss, but as a loving touch, that night when the herbal tonic company organized the free film screening at the soccer field.

But her departure didn't set Margio free. Whenever Maharani was on vacation she would come home, always hoping Margio would be there, hoping to have him to herself. Instead of loosening, the cords bound them together ever more firmly. On their date-like little rendezvous, Maharani would tell him about all the things she had seen at university in such a way that the stories felt like Margio's, too. At this point Maharani hadn't gotten used to holding his hand when they walked side by side, although everyone they knew talked about the young lovers. As Major Sadrah's wife put it: "That girl is crazy about Margio."

Now, on the night of the Tonic Company's film screening, the girl was impatient to make sure that Margio knew about the love rooted firmly in her body, and it was clear to Margio that the girl was his, although the awkwardness and discomfort still constrained him. Maharani remained an untouchable beauty.

They stepped away from the peanut vendor and walked to a grassy mound where people sat during football matches, under the lush shadow of a tropical almond tree. They sat close, and Margio could smell her scent. Her hair stroked his face when the wind impishly pulled at it. He still couldn't believe she had confessed her love for him, a confirmation that the oval face, still glowing in the darkness, might be his, a masterpiece in his possession. He was stunned.

Maharani took Margio's hand, lifted it, and coiled it round her body. He was holding the girl clumsily now, unsure whether to hold her tight, bringing the skin of his wrist against her bare waist, or simply hang onto her sweater. She lowered her head, and looped her own arm around Margio, bringing them closer together, their breathing finding a single rhythm. This is what it feels like to belong—the thought dawned on them almost simultaneously, as the gods of love hummed above their heads.

Down on the field, there was some kind of dispute. People were yelling. Night had deepened, and the crowd was tired of buying tonics. They wanted prizes. The voluble salesman, who had been handing out tonics as though the company were his, apologized and made the excuse that he still had buyers to serve and that no one had yet won the television set. If truth be told, the television set was a display item that would never actually change hands, though it was a charm far more alluring than the man's frothy mouth behind the microphone. Then, after handling the last of the transactions, he shut the doors on the pickup, only to reopen them when the time came to replace the film reel. The projector's light now fell on the white screen, which waved slightly in the wind, while people clapped and others whistled.

The film was the old classic *Cintaku di Kampus Biru*, famous for its provocative kissing scenes.

Margio and Maharani didn't pay much attention, not only because the screen was far away and the sound drowned by the audience's excited voices. They were too occupied with interpreting their bodies as they leant against each other, exchanging warmth as the air grew thick. It looked as if there would be heavy rain that night. Margio could feel the blood rushing faster in Maharani's body, just like in his own.

Maharani stirred a little and looked up at Margio's stubbly chin. She stared at him fixedly, as if something were moving on his face. Breathless, he realized it was time to act as a man and a lover. He returned that interrogating gaze of hers, their faces close, breathing the same air, feeling the breath on their faces, while their chests heaved in unison. The girl's eyes, shaded under curved lashes, dimmed by the light from street lamps and the cloud-swathed moon, looked at him longingly, and Margio knew what she wanted, but not what to do.

The girl was exasperated by his stupidity. Maharani was on the hunt, and Margio nearly choked, but tried to keep his

147

pride intact by waiting for the girl's lips to touch his. They had no idea how to begin, but pressed their mouths together, exchanging warmth and feeling the silkiness of each other's tongue.

They stopped abruptly—feeling conspicuous on the soccer field, though no one was watching—and stared at each other. The girl's eyes twinkled, and Margio looked sad. "There's something you don't know," he said forlornly, so softly the words went unheard. Pain welled up at the thought that despite their new intimacy, he couldn't share his deepest anguish. Maharani became uncomfortable. He was detached, and she sat up, no longer leaning on his shoulder. The pain in Margio increased, but he was afraid to lose the girl he worshiped. Maharani threw him a look of bewilderment, which was only translated when she opened her mouth.

"Don't you like me?"

The question pierced him. Of course he did. More than heaven or earth, he worshiped Maharani. He wanted her, but was shackled by the thought he didn't deserve her.

"I'm nervous," he whispered.

It set him free for a while. Maharani seemed to like the idea, *I'm nervous*. His insecurity smacked of romance. After all, they should be nervous. She was, too, and together they would cope with what was before them and grow in confidence. As they sat there, Maharani melting against him once more, his discomfort returned. He had lied about his nerves. The problem had a different complexion. It kept him from embracing her fiery love—it made him curse his inability to be honest with her.

Maharani came home the day after Margio's return, perhaps having heard of Komar bin Syueb's death. She said she was on vacation. Margio believed that, vacation or no, the girl had come back to comfort him, to sweep away his grief. Of course, she had misunderstood the situation. Margio wasn't sad at all.

Maharani visited his home every day, sometimes to eat with the family, her presence a reminder of the old days when Margio ate at Anwar Sadat's house. They grew closer, reaffirming the attraction founded between them a long time ago. One day Maharani asked him to take her to Komar's grave, misinterpreting his feelings. But Margio firmly said no. Maharani began to remember the old stories everyone told her about Komar bin Syueb's cruelty. She had seen it for herself when he whacked little Margio with a clothes-drying pole. She sensed for the first time the long history of pain behind Margio, and she wanted her love to be a balm and consolation to him.

Margio had left not long after Marian's death to avoid killing Komar. As he had told Mameh, there was a tiger inside him, and he had yet to learn how to control it. He left with the circus performers, following them to a town an hour's ride away. He had persuaded the manager to give him odd jobs, such as feeding the elephants and horses. The circus manager took one look at his strong build and imploring eyes and granted his wish, and the boy proved able to handle diligently a variety of tasks. Margio's real purpose was simply to see how the trainers tamed their tigers, to spy on their training sessions, to get to know these people for a couple of weeks. But as the shows came to an end and the circus troupe was about to head out to towns that stretched all the way east, Margio saw that his mission was doomed. The circus tigers were different from the one inside him.

He got his money for two weeks' work and said goodbye to the circus. He stayed put, wanting to keep up to date with the news from home. He couldn't uproot himself completely, even though his father dominated his memories of the town. He missed his mother and Mameh, and once in a while Maharani's beautiful face drifted into his mind's eye, as would, with less frequency, his friends, Agus Sofyan's stall, the surau, and the nightwatch hut—he couldn't possibly lose them all. So there he stayed, and told bus drivers and their assistants not to tell anyone where he was, devouring whatever news they brought.

Until one afternoon a bus driver told him his father was dead, and his body had started to rot.

He got on that bus, sat by an open window and let the sea breeze that blew through rows of pandanus hit his face. During the ride, his mind wandered, picturing his father's rotting body at his feet. For Margio nothing was more miraculous than to hear that Komar bin Syueb had died without himself having to cut his throat.

He got off the bus just as the truck carrying the boar hunters arrived, and his pulse beat faster on realizing he had missed an exciting hunt. Dozens of leashed ajaks leapt off the truck, milling on the sidewalk until someone dragged them to Major Sadrah's house on the side of the road right next to the military headquarters. Two fat hogs, with empty eyes and tied by the feet, hung from bamboo poles suspended on the shoulders of four boys. The ajaks are going to be happy when the day of the boar fight arrives, he thought. Once the hogs are dead, the pork eaters will go for a feast at the Chinese restaurants by the beach. He smelt the familiar stench of mud. Margio simply waved, paying particular attention to

Major Sadrah, because Komar bin Syueb was yet to be buried and to socialize would be unseemly.

When he found out that Komar bin Syueb was going to be buried next to Marian, he didn't like the idea. Mameh insisted it was their father's last wish, for whatever that was worth. When he saw she was serious, he gave in and let fate have its way. Little Marian would have her revenge regardless of where his old man lay, and Komar would be slain every day in Hell for all eternity. He went to the surau because Komar had been brought there, and took part in the prayers for the dead. When Kyai Jahro asked him if he wanted to see Komar's face, Margio promptly shook his head, worried that, should he agree, his father might awaken from death.

Before shouldering the coffin, Margio received from Mameh the basket of flower petals. He wondered what good flowers would be for this rotting beast. But once again he saw Mameh's eyes begging him to spread the petals over the casket, instead of tossing them into the gutter. It dawned on Margio that Mameh had to be the sanest of them all. Her heart was earnest and free of hate, and when he looked at her, he was flooded with bittersweet memories of their childhood together. Perhaps they would be straightforwardly happy with their father consigned to Hell.

Kyai Jahro chanted prayers, and some muddy boys from the truck joined the funeral procession, escorting the coffin. Margio, walking at the back, scooped up some flowers and threw them over the coffin. Despite the colorful petals, the mood grew increasingly somber, below the clamor of people singing praise for the Prophet. They walked in rows on a path through the parched cacao plantation, heading to the Budi Darma cemetery, under the rays of late-afternoon sun

151

that were beginning to turn everything red. The tiger writhed inside Margio, but Margio whispered to it softly: "Look, the guy is dead, so please rest." He kept on scooping up the petals, tossing them into the air, and this time they floated about as though unwilling to fall, as though mirroring the thrower's reluctance. Eventually, they alighted on the sandy path to be trampled underfoot.

The gravedigger had been waiting in all patience, chin propped on his spade's handle, puffing on a hand-rolled cigarette. Mameh was right. The gaping grave lay next to Marian's mound. Margio recalled her burial and planting the headstone above the resting-place of that tiny body. He stood beside her now, trickling a handful of petals on her, and an unexpected surge of emotion brought him close to tears.

They lowered the casket and lifted the lid, showing Komar bin Syueb blanketed in a shroud that looked like a barber's bib. Kyai Jahro was chanting prayers incomprehensible to Margio, who had never quite finished his Koran lessons, having read through the Arabic verses without ever grasping their meaning. He set the basket on the mound and raised his hands with the palms open, saying amen repeatedly just like the others. Kyai Jahro ended the prayers, the mourners said the final amen, rubbed their faces with both palms, and the gravedigger descended into the burial pit, telling Margio to come help. Margio rolled up his pants, hurried down, and stood beside the gravedigger, feeling the wet soil under his feet, the ground that would become his father's final home.

Two of his friends lifted Komar out the casket, and then handed him to Margio and the gravedigger. The body was really heavy, perplexing Margio who had seen him old and frail and had heard about his many illnesses. Still the body weighed a ton. His two friends above had felt it, and he had seen surprise in their faces. Now it was the turn of the gravedigger and Margio. They staggered a little, panting, bracing themselves against the weight to lay Komar in his grave.

The pit was too small, preventing Komar from being laid out full-length. "For God's sake," said the gravedigger, "I measured it." Margio noticed it too, and estimated that it could need to be at least a foot longer. With some difficulty, they hauled up the body, the shroud slipping haphazardly, and put it back in the casket. Margio waited at one corner of the burial pit, while the gravedigger sourly asked for his spade and then got to work. He did the job hurriedly, tossing the earth every which way. It was getting late, and the cemetery was drenched red in the evening sun.

They once more lowered Komar's corpse, which had grown even weightier. How this happened was anybody's guess. But the four people carrying the corpse felt the change, as if something were swelling inside it. Margio thought it must be the weight of the man's sins, and he quietly scowled at the very idea shouldering his father's sins himself. Together with the gravedigger he dropped the body carelessly, sparing his own back.

Another problem. This time the grave was too narrow. Had the body expanded or did the grave somehow narrow in width as the gravedigger lengthened it? "Goddamnit," the gravedigger said, really angry this time. "This soil doesn't want him." Margio and the man strained to heave the corpse back into the casket before the pit was dug broader. They lowered him again, and again the space was too small. They dug more, and it was still too narrow, as if the pit walls were closing in, refusing to swallow the body.

Beaten down with fatigue, the gravedigger's face was pale in the evening light. Margio was red with fury. They all looked at Kyai Jahro, who stood on an earthen mound, and he was chanting prayers in a low voice, begging the Judge to accept the body, for the living didn't wish it to rot unburied. As he pursued his muffled prayers, leaves fell and the wind grew strong. The kyai closed his eyes, still moving his lips, then reopened them to stare at the body confined below. He turned to the crowd and said, "Bury him whatever way you can."

They stuck Komar bin Syueb in there, not caring how tight the space was, the dead man curled into a crouch like a sleeping dog. Even Margio pitied him. Maybe that is what he deserves, thought the boy, gazing at a body that might have been doubled up in pain. He and the gravedigger wedged the body with clumps of earth so it couldn't roll over. The pair planted the supporting planks, one by one, covering the contours of the white shroud. The planks served as a powerful barrier between the world of the living and the realm of the dead, where Komar bin Syueb was confined.

It was almost dark when the sandy red soil finally covered him. The gravedigger slowly stepped on this soil, but didn't make it too compact, as a mandatory precaution lest the dead should be resurrected. Besides, it would make things easier if he had to dig there again. He embedded the tombstone, bearing the man's name alongside that of his father, and spread tiny pebbles around it. Moved by a strange pang of pity, Margio planted a frangipani tree at one end of the grave, and scattered the remaining flower petals, which exuded the scent of roses, jasmine, and ylang-ylang. Komar bin Syueb was left there with the sea breezes and ghosts.

154

As the air became still, they returned carrying the empty casket, treading the path back home with hurried steps. Sweat poured down Margio's forehead, but he wasn't tired and his spirits began to lift. Again and again he told himself, "Think about it, the beast is dead, so now it is up to us how to live our lives."

At home, Mameh told him their mother had slapped her, and Margio wondered if Komar bin Syueb had bequeathed his brutality to Nuraeni. When he heard Mameh's explanation, he couldn't help but stifle a laugh. Mameh's suggestion was sound. It might be good for her to remarry. She was still young. How old now? Not even forty, Margio thought, too soon to be shelved away as a widow. He would support any man who wished to take her as a wife, provided he wasn't like Komar and promised never to be cruel. Margio would do anything for Nuraeni's peace of mind, and just like Mameh, he had thought of letting her remarry. That said, it was hardly proper to suggest it on the very day her husband was buried. No matter how much Nuraeni hated Komar, her daughter's impudent mouth was just asking for a whack. Margio told Mameh that, as time passed, their mother would be cured of her craziness and she would be her old sweet self again.

Mameh wanted Margio to butcher Komar's remaining chickens. He was reluctant at first, unable to comprehend why she would bother preparing a ritual meal for a man even the earth had rejected. He didn't tell her what had happened at the cemetery, worried it would only add to her grief, but he was still disinclined to help her organize a prayer ceremony for the vilest man he had ever known. But Mameh insisted, reminding him that every human being needed prayers, and that Komar did leave a few chickens and rabbits behind. Margio relented and he slit their throats one by one as Mameh got things ready in the kitchen.

It reminded Margio of the times he would steal Komar's chickens in petty revenge. Komar probably knew who the thief was, but by this point Margio was a young man in his late teens, and his father didn't dare challenge him. Mameh certanly knew who the culprit was.

The chickens butchered, Mameh brought out a bucket of hot water in which to soak them. She got busy plucking, while in the kitchen the stove had been lit to heat the water for simmering the meat. The rice was ready, and it seemed that Mameh had cooked while everyone else had been at the Budi Darma cemetery. Nuraeni showed up in the doorway to watch what they were up to, exactly at the moment when Ma Soma started chanting the call to the dusk prayers from the surau. The expression on her face was cold. After Marian's death she had become withdrawn, and now that Komar had fallen, she was even more reticent. Margio turned to look at her, and all he could do was beg the cosmos to give her a little taste of joy of the kind she had known when Marian was born.

The baby had been ailing since birth, its body no bigger than one of his calves, its head a bit larger. It had sunken cheeks and a protruding chin, and looked rather like a stick insect. Margio didn't notice this at first, because the baby was kept tightly wrapped in red swaddling clothes and its little blanket gave the impression that it was fat. Then one morning Mameh came with a pail of lukewarm water and Nuraeni unwrapped the baby to reveal its miserable self. It no longer wailed before dawn, but just lay there with its eyes half closed.

"Looks like she's going to die," Nuraeni said.

Her breasts didn't produce much milk, and what they did seemed drained by the baby's first suckling. Kasia came late in the afternoon with bottled milk, but the newborn merely gave it a reluctant nip, parting and shutting her lips as the milk dribbled down her cheeks. Her breathing came in little gasps, sometimes she cried softly, but mostly she was quiet, as if it was written in the stars that she would grow up to be an obedient little girl. Margio sat in a chair beside his mother's bed, anxiously observing the fragile little being, exchanging glances with Nuraeni and Mameh as they all wondered in their hearts if this creature would see another day.

Margio breathed in the damp, foul air of the room, still fetid from the birth. The wickerwork ceiling was stained with water. The whitewash was peeling, and up there the spiders persistently built their webs. A small reddish light bulb shone weakly. Clothes were piled up on the corner of the mattress and inside a basket. Mameh's old school bag lay on the top of the cabinet and her unused shoes were stuffed under the bed. For Margio, circumstances had conspired to smother the little baby.

He stood up and asked for permission to open the windows. Nuraeni and Mameh were apparently of the same mind, and so Margio let in the light from the yard, and fresh air surged into the room bringing a little warmth and the scent of leaves, flowers, and loose soil. Spots of light landed on the baby, and Mameh moved the infant, fearing it would overheat. Yet the little one remained half asleep, as if unaware of the exquisite cosmos arriving to greet her.

"Looks like she's going to die," Nuraeni repeated. The woman's sadness swept away any memory of the pleasure

157

she had taken in this child. She had stopped chanting lulla-
bies, and her hands no longer stroked the baby's sparse hair.
She was looking at it wistfully, perhaps knowing that the
baby's death was fated, and seeing how the little one's soul
was already departing from its body. Margio couldn't bear to
watch both the baby and its mother. He left the room and
with it the process of death and the profound defeat of a
despairing mother.

Komar bin Syueb had not come home that day, and Margio
was seriously thinking of beheading him. Evidently he hadn't
gone to work, as the shaving kit was still in his room. But
both his bike and his favorite purebred rooster had gone.
Margio realized that the day before his father had left for the
cockfighting arena in the ruins of the railway station, and
God only knew where he had slept last night.

The station wasn't far from House 131, just a few hundred
yards to the rear. Margio was on his way there, with his hands
sunk into his pockets. He passed a row of houses, nodded a
short greeting when he ran into a friend, and took a shortcut
through the brick factory until he arrived at the steel rails.
For a long time the railroad had been out of use, its wooden
planks decayed, its steel bars rusted, and part of it had
drowned in a rolling sea of knee-high weeds. Some nearby
households used the rails to dry out mattresses, while others
did the same for rows of firewood, letting them bake in the
heat. Still others would roll out their tarpaulins to shower
their unhusked grains of harvested rice with sunlight.
Herders let their sheep and cows graze on the wild grasses,
yet the plants never perished since they grew faster than the
animals could consume them.

Margio remembered when the railway still operated, back

in the early days after the family relocated. It was a dead-end route—a few miles to the west the train would reach its terminus. The railway used only one train, going back and forth, and thanks to this it could stop any time it pleased without worrying about collisions. The joke went that one passenger always asked to be dropped in front of his house instead of at the station, while another hailed the train to stop so he could get on board, and sometimes the engine driver had to hit the brake as the track was covered in firewood or resting cows, which had to be removed for the journey to continue. This joke was based entirely on truth, so far as the townsfolk were concerned. Then one day the train stopped coming, with no prior announcement or explanation, like a girl who silently ditches her boyfriend.

The station chief was still around, although no one knew if he'd retired or was still waiting for the ghost train's return. He lived next to the ruined station building, and people still referred to him as Station Chief. The building itself was nothing but bare bones. Piece by piece, it had lost all its equipment save for its timeless bell and the station's signboard. The ticket office was home to a wicker mattress used by various prostitutes, and the platform was crammed with dovecotes and chicken cages. Such was the palace of the cockfights and pigeon races. Every sunny afternoon, rows of birds could be seen flying faster than the train ever had. Elsewhere, the roosters would cavort, testing their spurs on each other.

When Margio arrived, it was too early for the usual hustle and bustle. All he found was a homeless mother and her child sat on a piece of cardboard, a dog rummaging in the garbage.

There was no one to ask about Komar's whereabouts. Disgruntled, Margio leaned on the bar of a crossing gate. The bastard should be here, he thought, inspecting the splatters of chicken and pigeon guano on the platform as if searching for traces of Komar's purebred rooster. People came walking up a path that crossed the railway track, pushing their bikes, carrying dark green bananas and sacks filled with who-knows-what, seemingly headed for the market. Women clutched their baskets on their way back from shopping. He kicked the gravel before leaving, walking on one rail and trying to keep his balance.

When the train ceased to run, he had stopped hanging out here. Back when he had found the billowing dark smoke from the locomotive's chimney fascinating, Margio would spend whole afternoons watching it go by. When the train was being turned around in the shunting yard, he joined the other cheerful little boys, who climbed on board and dangled fearlessly from the locomotive as it rotated. At other times, hearing the sound of the distant train, he would put a nine-inch nail on one track to get it flattened by the fearsome wheels. That way he'd have a small knife that only needed a little filing to make it really sharp. Some old men spotted what he was doing and tried to scare him by saying that he might make the train run off the track. Margio didn't believe them, and he went on as before. One day the train hit a fat cow, and instead of running off course, it nearly split the cow in half.

These days, Komar ruled the station with his gambler friends. As Nuraeni became increasingly crazy, the flower jungle appeared, and his wife's willingness to share his bed vanished, Komar resorted to this sanctuary. Almost every

160

afternoon, after returning from his stall and hurling his bike at a cluster of roses, he'd carry his purebred rooster to the arena. Under a mercury lamp still glowing from the time of the station's heyday, he would hang about until late in the night, watching the games, feeding his rooster, or bathing it with what he called a herbal concoction.

No one in the house was interested in this business of his, and since Komar's infatuation with the rooster had made him less violent at home, they were not inclined to complain. His animalistic instincts were apparently channeled into cock-fights, and the occupants of number 131 found a little peace as a result, until the day Komar learnt his wife was pregnant and went berserk. After that, he spent even more time at the station. Someone said he had seen Komar sleep there, perhaps with a prostitute in that ticket office, and Margio couldn't care less. The more Komar wasn't home, the better. Nuraeni had suffered enough at his hands.

There was no sign of him there, although he had left home with his purebred. Perhaps he had fallen out with someone, who would slit his throat, chop up his body, and put it in a sack with a bunch of rocks before throwing it into the river. Komar would be gone forever, and the thought gave Margio a thrill as he sluggishly walked along the track and through the brick factory to get home.

At number 131, he found the strapping rooster in the front yard. A rock held its cage steady against the wind. The man himself slumped in a chair inside, smoking a clove cigarette. This annoyed Margio immensely, and he tried to mock him, asking, "To what do we owe the pleasure, sir?" But after seeing the tired wrinkled face, a different grief crept into his soul, as he looked at the man who had seen, or would soon see, the death of an infant who was not his daughter though born to his wife.

Margio sat far across from him, staring without a word, before turning his face toward the room where Nuraeni forlornly contemplated the dying baby. He then turned his gaze back toward Komar, rusting away in his old age. The family was now complete, everyone present and all its fractures and hatreds accounted for. This couldn't be good. Komar glanced at Margio, briefly, unable to counter the boy's gaze, and then returned his attention to the clove cigarette between his fingers. Margio stared blankly, his eyes half closed, not sure what he was thinking, and focused solely on his own breathing. Mameh was the only one to stir. She carried the water bucket back into the kitchen, before returning to the room to sit on the edge of the bed. Nuraeni looked up at Margio, also very briefly, before staring at the baby who had started to fall asleep, probably never to reawaken.

It was still alive when a new day came, though it moved less than ever. Its mother's milk had dried up, and the infant only gave Kasia's bottle a brief lick despite Nuraeni's efforts to force some of the liquid into its mouth. The sockets of its eyes had deepened, and its mouth drooped. The smell of death emanated from it, like steam from a pot of hot rice.

The baby fought the angel of death, and Komar wouldn't look at it. Not once had he entered the room from which it never emerged, the mother fearing what the wind might do to such a tiny body. The cruel father merely sat in his chair smoking his clove cigarettes. Should his stomach insist on being filled, he would go to the kitchen and eat alone, without requesting or offering anything. Margio didn't move much. He slept in his chair and forgot about his friends. He watched events at home as if he were watching a play, coolly interested in how the actors performed the roles assigned them.

At nine Komar left for his stall, and relative peace followed, though Nuraeni didn't cease to fret over the little one. It wasn't the baby's life that Margio was worried about. If the half-living doll died, he was sure his mother would descend even further into madness. He wished Komar would do something—regardless of the baby's paternity—for Nuraeni, instead of just fussing over his rooster. But it was clear to everyone that Komar was glad the child was wasting away, eager for it to die.

On the seventh day, the man went missing. The rest of the family was overjoyed that the baby had survived so long on the few drops of bottled milk it managed to lick from the bottle. Nuraeni, Mameh, and Margio began to feel hopeful. A week was a milestone. If the baby could make it this far, it might tough it out for a year, a decade, or longer, even though its tiny frame was no stronger and its breathing imperceptible. Margio caught something like a smile on Nuraeni's face, and the woman found the courage to bring her baby out of the bedroom, tighly wound as ever to defend it against the elements.

This was when Komar should have named the baby. The child had been born in his home, after all, and for all the neighbors knew it was his. Instead, he went missing, leaving no word of his whereabouts. Margio searched for him again, but had no success. Neither the shaving kit nor the fighting rooster had gone. Since early morning Nuraeni had seated herself on the chair at the front of the house, singing a soothing lullaby as she softly rocked the baby on her lap. "Soon you will have a name," she whispered. But Komar was gone, and there was no sign he would be coming back.

It was Mameh who told Margio to shave the baby. Without any of the usual ceremony, with only his sister and mother in attendance, he opened his father's shaving kit to find a pair of scissors and a razor. The baby was still half asleep in Nuraeni's lap. Her mother removed the baby's cap, and Margio washed its thin hair. With two fingers of one hand he took a lock of soot-black hair, and with the other opened the scissors to start cutting. A piece of paper on the table caught the strands. Afterward, they would weigh the baby's hair and, in accordance with tradition, make a gift of that much rice to a pauper. Margio and Mameh watched each follicle carefully to ensure nothing was lost.

The ritual was over in ten minutes, and Nuraeni's eyes were glazed with happiness. She slipped a knitted cap once again over the baby's bald head to protect it from the menacing air. Margio suggested his mother give the baby a name, and she chose Marian. The name popped out just like that. It could have been the name of a character from one of the radio dramas Nuraeni listened to in the afternoons, when their next-door neighbor put his radio on a chair in his front yard, and people squatted around it to listen. Or perhaps it recalled the name of a girl she knew in her youth. Margio and Mameh didn't ask. That the baby had a name was enough.

She died later that day, before they had finished eating the prized fighting rooster Margio had vengefully butchered. The baby went without a sound, simply fading away, the twilight of its life giving way to darkness. Nuraeni walked into her jungle garden, doing her best to keep her body steady. She picked flowers, chanting sad songs, her eyes flooded with tears.

What Maharani didn't know was that there was a deep wound within Margio's family, and the dead girl touched every part of it. That night at the film screening, the question of whether to tell her who Marian's father was, and that it was impossible for them to be lovers, tortured Margio. He wanted to lance the boil, to show her the true horror of the facts, but was deterred by his admiration for her and the girl's relentless expressions of love while they embraced in a corner of the soccer field. They kissed, and the truth froze Margio to the core.

The girl could tell he was uneasy, and put it down to nerves and inexperience. When she touched him teasingly, trying to free him from self-consciousness, he only looked at her with anguished eyes, pained with the knowledge that losing her was inevitable, and wondering if he could bring himself to break things off.

He couldn't possibly tell her what he had seen one particular day not long after Komar bin Syueb had found out about Nuraeni's pregnancy and had beaten her half to death. That day, once her husband had gone, she had rallied. She sang and beautified herself. Her good mood was inexplicable to Margio, even perverse. There were bruises on her body, but she didn't seem to feel them, and he was amazed by his mother's endurance. Nuraeni looked fresh, more pampered than abused. She wore a beige dress, and rushed out of the house despite her protuberant belly. Margio followed secretly, and when she reached Anwar Sadat's house, he lay down out of sight to keep watch. By then he had started to suspect Anwar Sadat, whose wickedness and roving eye were well known, and of course Nuraeni spent almost as much time at his place as she did at home. Margio wanted evidence, though he had no idea what he would do if he got it.

Dragging his feet, he crept closer to the familiar house. He entered through the side door without knocking, as he had done many times over the years. He found himself on the central porch where clothes were hanging out to dry. His mother would normally be doing laundry at the well or preparing lunch. The house was quiet, and there was no sign of life. Margio walked in without making any noise, his eyes fixed on a painting hanging on the wall. Maesa Dewi was in her room with her baby, the door slightly ajar. He went to the kitchen, but no one was there. Turning, he stood in front of Anwar Sadat's bedroom door. He wanted to open it, but couldn't. He chose to leave.

On the house's western side, there was a raised bed about six feet square, bordered by a waist-high wall. The family grew oranges and bananas there, below the house's many broad windows. The yard was taboo to outsiders, except for Margio, who had often gone there to chop down withered banana leaves. Through the front bedroom window, he could see the room was empty. Laila wasn't there. As he had already observed, lazy Maesa Dewi lay under a blanket despite the daylight flooding her bedroom. The third window, which was Maharani's, was always closed, opening only when the girl came home on vacation. Margio paused by the next room.

He heard muffled grunts from inside, and there was no doubt in his mind that Anwar Sadat and his mother were making love. Curiosity, or perhaps mischief, drove him closer, despite already knowing the truth. Through a glass window swathed by a crimson curtain, he saw his naked mother under Anwar Sadat. Unaware of the peeping Tom, their bodies rocked, intimate and inseparable. Margio wanted to see his mother's expression at that moment, to know the brilliant hues of her sweaty face, on which twenty years of abuse had been washed away by passion. He was happy to see them absorbed in lovemaking. His gaze strayed over the twisting bodies, dissolving into one another, before good sense finally prompted him to step away and walk home. He needed to sit down and clear his mind. On the way back, a headache surged up more feverishly than any hangover. He wanted to cry.

Later that afternoon, at the nightwatch hut, he started drinking everything he could get his hands on, mostly bottles of beer mixed with arak from Agus Sofyan's stall. Lying there vomiting and coughing, he raved about a damned woman and a bloodthirsty fox. His friends couldn't make head nor tail of any of this. And he rambled on: "For that smile, I'll forgive you for sleeping with any bastard." He almost went mad thinking about the chaos in his family, until in a moment of strange epiphany he took his mother's side. He couldn't deny her a little happiness.

After Marian's death and his mother's spiraling sadness, Margio longed for his father's head. The man finally showed up, basking in victory, not long after the burial. But Margio couldn't find the courage to take a machete to his father. The memory of Nuraeni's and Anwar Sadat's naked bodies restrained him, making him pity his father, despite the old man's loathsome arrogance. But the urge to put an end to Komar's life wouldn't abate. On the morning he met his tigress, it was intense. He could feel it boiling inside, a goad to the beast, who wanted to leap at Komar bin Syueb's throat.

Rage gripped him even more tightly when he faced Maharani, who showed up the day after Komar's death. Margio was on the verge of celebrating the family's liberation, looking forward to a glorious life without his brute of a father. But then he ran into Maharani that night and she confessed her love for him. He would have to tell her everything, to put an end to any idea of the two of them being together. The longer he delayed, the harder it would be to come clean.

The second reel began, which meant they'd been sitting holding each other, exchanging timid kisses for nearly an hour. Margio's awkwardness was driving Maharani to distraction. She broke off her latest attempt at a kiss and looked at him accusingly, silently demanding an explanation. Filled with guilt and shame, Margio braced himself, ready to be punished for a crime he hadn't committed.

"Tell me, don't you like me?" she said, and her shoulders began to shudder. Hearing her sobs, Margio faced her and held her hands, but she pushed him away. Margio reached for her shoulders, but she backed off. It was no pretense; she was distraught. There was no easy way out for Margio.

"There's something you don't know," he said. This time his voice sounded clear, determined. Maharani continued to cry. His cryptic declaration didn't interest her. Whatever he said, it would lead to the same conclusion: their relationship was a waste of time; the kisses, the tenderness between them meant nothing; her feelings didn't touch him. He didn't want her, and that was that.

"It's impossible for us to love each other," he said.
"Why?"
She looked him in the eye, her nose red and wet. Sodden hair stuck to her cheeks. Looking at her made him shrink

168

inside, lamenting all that was now unraveling, wishing away what his mother had done so he could hold her, kiss her. But Maharani was staring a challenge at him, demanding an answer. There was no going back on what he had started.

Margio grunted, and what he said next tumbled rapidly off his tongue:

"Your father slept with my mother, and a little girl named Marian was born. She died on the seventh day of her life, because my father found out and beat my mother so badly that Marian was born prematurely."

It was enough to cut off the girl's sobs. Instead, she gaped at words she was at first unable to digest. She only knew Margio had uttered a truth as significant as any Koranic lesson from Kyai Jahro's sermons, which echoed through the town on Friday afternoons through the mosque's loudspeaker.

Maharani stood up, her eyes locked on Margio the way she might squint at a liar. She stuttered, longing to say something, but gave up and merely bit her lip. Margio returned her stare, silently attesting to the truth of what he'd said. He didn't have to describe the window where he had seen the two lovers wrestling to inflame each other. In the simple steadiness of his gaze Maharani could judge his words, and she walked away from him. She crossed the street without bothering to look out for cars that might smash her to pieces, her flared jeans flapping as she charged forward. Wiping her eyes, unable to stop crying, she headed home. This was the night his daughter would baffle Anwar Sadat with her strange behavior, locking herself in her room until morning and then fleeing the house.

Margio went home before the movie ended and felt relief, even though the pain of losing the girl was excruciating. He sat on the front porch, looking at his mother's flower jungle, and swore that all the misfortunes of his life had to come to an end. Two hearts were broken, but it couldn't be any other way. He was still there when the night was at its darkest, and a light rain washed the earth. There was a fresh, reassuring breeze, bearing the scent of damp dust. Mameh opened the door and told him to come inside, but Margio stayed put, spinning in a whirlpool of speculation and reflections.

The rain fell harder, water overflowing the gutters. He hoped the sky would exhaust itself, and the next day would be dry for the boar hunt. The memory of his hunts brought him back to life, and he foresaw brilliant days ahead. He had the tigress, his loathsome father was gone, and so was Maharani, who had become a burden. Mameh and their mother were all he needed at home.

He stayed up all night. The rain had stopped come morning, but the winds blew, and something in the turbulent air told him Maharani had left the village. He toyed with the idea of seeing her, to make peace. She wasn't to blame for what had happened. Fate had done it all. A drifting scent told him the girl still brimmed with tears, as she hurriedly carried her bags to the bus terminal, refusing to let Anwar Sadat see her off. Margio ought to be at her side, as he had been when they huddled under the umbrella. He should carry her bags, help her up onto the bus, tell her he would be there for her when she returned, and wave when the engine roared and the wheels turned on the asphalt. But that was a daydream, and in real life everything was lost. All that remained was a precious lesson that love causes pain, and the conviction that it couldn't be otherwise.

His eyes were bloodshot, but he had no desire to sleep.

Mameh and Nuraeni had woken up. Mameh was creating a hubbub in the kitchen, her kingdom for the past few years, while Nuraeni sat in her chair drinking the sweet, steaming coffee her daughter had prepared. She looked shriveled, even more wrinkled than during the sad years she lived under Komar's fist. Marian's death had been the greatest blow, more agonizing than the hard rattan duster. Margio looked at her and wondered if Komar's death released them at all, whether the suffering he had created would ever really end. The answer was in a face that resembled a cracked riverbed.

Margio snacked on a piece of tofu he found lying on the dining table and wandered outside, to feel the warmth of the rising sun. Maharani was certainly on her way. He could see Anwar Sadat in his shorts and ABC jewelry store undershirt at the pancake stall, complaining about his daughter. They exchanged glances, and in his heart Margio knew this was the only person who could make his mother happy. Margio didn't stop by the stall, and walked instead to Major Sadrah's house to play with the ajaks. He liked to play with the animals, getting them to skip around him, but his mind would circle back to Nuraeni and Anwar Sadat nonetheless, and he was on edge.

He walked the narrow alleys of the township, meeting friends without exchanging many words. He didn't go home that day. He ate only guavas picked from the pawnshop's front yard, and bummed a cigarette off Agung Yuda. He had intended to sleep at the nightwatch hut, but his eyes wouldn't close. Strange thoughts about his mother made him restless.

He wanted to talk with his pal Agung Yuda, but embarrassment and shame deterred him. The two of them clowned around in the soccer field before lying down to watch pigeons

171

flutter in the depths of the sky. Then he dragged his friend to Agus Sofyan's stall. Even there he couldn't get the news off his chest. Instead he tortured himself with thoughts of Maharani, who could listen and talk to him without constraint.

At the end of his day's wanderings, he found himself stranded in Anwar Sadat's front yard. He was unarmed, and had no intention of killing the man. He only wanted to talk. What made him hesitate was embarrassment, not fear. When he saw the door open and spotted Anwar Sadat, still in the clothes he had worn that morning, appearing exactly as imagined, Margio went to him. He had to speak while he had the courage.

"I know you slept with my mother and Marian was your daughter," he said.

The declaration hung in the air. Anwar Sadat was ashen-faced.

"Marry my mother and she'll be happy."

Anwar Sadat shook his head nervously, and his reply came out brokenly.

"That's impossible, you know I have a wife and daughters." Something in his face said the proposition was absurd, making what he said next redundant. "Besides, I don't love your mother."

That was when the tiger came out of Margio, white as a swan.

Acknowledgements

I would like to thank Tariq Ali and Benedict Anderson for all their help and advice as early readers of this translation.

E. K.